The Wolf's Mate Book 7: Lindy & The Wulfen

R. E. Butler

Copyright 2014 R. E. Butler

The Wolf's Mate Book 7
Lindy & The Wulfen
by R. E. Butler

License Notes

This book is licensed for your personal enjoyment only. This book may not be re-sold or given away to other people. If you would like to share this book with another person, please purchase an additional copy for each recipient. If you're reading this book and did not purchase it, or it was not purchased for your use only, then please purchase your own copy. Thank you for respecting the hard work of the author.

Cover by Ramona Lockwood

This book is a work of fiction. Names, characters, places, and incidents are the product of the author's imagination and not to be construed as real. Any resemblance to actual persons, living or dead, events or locations is coincidental.

Disclaimer: The material in this book is for mature audiences only and contains graphic sexual content and is intended for those older than the age of 18 only.

ISBN: 1500190586
ISBN 13: 9781500190583

I'd like to sincerely thank Iliana Gkioni for her help with elements of this book. I so appreciate your knowledge, time, and friendship. XOXO

I'd like to thank Devin Govaere for editing this story.

Many thanks to Amanda Pederick for beta-reading, line editing, and being there for me when I thought bears were coming to stay in Allen.

Much love to my sisterfriend, Joyce.

To Aunt B. L. and my husband, B.B., I love you both.

Special thanks to the most awesome group of gals I've ever had the pleasure of knowing, the *Wild Shifter Babes Street Team*—you guys rock!

TABLE OF CONTENTS

Chapter One	1
Chapter Two	9
Chapter Three	14
Chapter Four	20
Chapter Five	38
Chapter Six	46
Chapter Seven	51
Chapter Eight	56
Chapter Nine	62
Chapter Ten	73
Chapter Eleven	82
Chapter Twelve	94
Chapter Thirteen	107
Chapter Fourteen	116
Chapter Fifteen	125
Chapter Sixteen	136
Chapter Seventeen	142
Chapter Eighteen	148
Chapter Nineteen	152
Chapter Twenty	164
Chapter Twenty One	171
Chapter Twenty Two	181
Chapter Twenty Three	196

Epilogue	201
Contact the Author	204
Other Works by R. E. Butler	205
Coming in 2014	207

Chapter One

Lindy was vaguely aware of the toilet flushing and groaned softly, turning over and burying her face in her pillow. Then she was *very* aware of two things. First, that she had rolled over onto underwear that was definitely not hers, and second, that someone had just flushed her toilet and she lived alone.

As she sat up and her head swam with a hangover to beat all hangovers, the previous night's activities came rushing back with alarming clarity.

Drinking at Jake's with Faith and McKenna to celebrate McKenna's impending mating.

Way too many Rum and Coke's.

Accepting a ride home from…oh fuck.

Someone sat down on the bed hard enough to bounce her in the air. Bruce Smith, a fellow Tressel Pack member, reached next to her for his underwear and gave her a smarmy smile as he lifted the briefs into the air. "Unless you want to keep these for a trophy?"

She stifled the desire to gag, but just barely.

Oh, how the hell had she fallen so low that she'd let Bruce not only take her home when she was drunk but also have sex with her?

He stood and pulled on his jeans and turned to face her as she sat staring numbly at him. He looked at her, his blue eyes regarding her for only a brief moment before he walked to the end of the bed, picked up his shirt and shoes, and walked out of her bedroom without a word.

It was just a few moments later that she heard the front door open and close. She hadn't even rated a goodbye from one of the biggest assholes in the pack. But she hadn't expected to be respected by a drunk one-nighter, had she? It's not like she was dating him, or ever would.

A little bit of anger rolled through her. Why had her best friends let her leave the bar with him? They all had firm no-asshole rules about going home with guys. Bruce was definitely on their asshole list.

She spied her cell on the nightstand and grabbed it, noticing it was only three a.m. Dialing McKenna, she was surprised when her friend didn't answer. As she dialed Faith, she stood slowly, waited for her stomach to stop rolling, and walked to the bathroom.

"What do you want?" Faith's frosty tone stopped Lindy in her tracks.

"What's wrong?"

"Are you serious? You have a lot of nerve calling me after that bullshit you pulled last night, Lindy. I'm too pissed to talk to you."

The call ended, and Lindy stood in her bathroom, naked, staring at the phone. What the hell had just happened?

Putting the phone on the counter, she clicked on the overhead light, squinted at the brightness, and reached into the shower to turn the water on. Finding aspirin in the medicine cabinet, she tossed back several and then drank a few glasses of cold water. As she put the cup down, her eyes strayed to the wastebasket, and she noticed a used condom inside it.

Well thank goodness!

At least she'd had enough sense in her stupor to have him wrap his dick. Shoving the unwanted thoughts of having sex with Bruce into the back of her mind, she stepped under the warm spray. As she poured rose-scented body wash onto a scrubby sponge and began to wash away the scent of Bruce from her skin, she replayed the evening over in her mind.

Earlier that day, Faith and McKenna had shown up at the bookstore where Lindy worked, and McKenna had proudly shown off the mating marks on the back of her neck from her boyfriend and fellow Tressel Pack member, Drake. Lindy had smiled and congratulated her friend, but inside she'd been green with envy. Not because of Drake. He was too young for Lindy's tastes. But jealous of her friend moving on with her life. The three girls had been best friends since preschool, and they'd had their share of arguments over the years. But what had bothered Lindy most was that McKenna hadn't been looking for a mate and had landed one. Sure he was young, but he had a steady job and was cute.

Over the course of their celebration, Lindy must have gotten a loose tongue and told McKenna her true feelings on the mating. Closing her eyes as she soaped her body, she tried to remember what she had said. All she really got from that experiment was more pounding in her head and a bit of dizziness that made her want to retch.

Letting the spray rinse the soap off her body, she shampooed her hair, then soaped her skin once more for good measure. She stepped out of the shower and wrapped a towel around her head and then another around her body. After brushing her teeth, she flipped off the light, and went back into her bedroom. Detouring past the bed, she headed down the hallway to the front door of her small ranch home and threw the deadbolt.

Sure, her pride was hurt that Bruce had walked out without any common courtesy, but she was glad he was gone. That tumbling into bed with him had come in some way because she had hurt both her best friends with some drunken tirade just made waking up with that slime ball even worse.

Blowing out a breath, she headed back to her bedroom to strip the bed and change the sheets before settling down for the night. She just hoped things would be better when she woke up.

After a few hours of sleep, Lindy woke up feeling less hung over and definitely glad to be the only one in her bed. She still didn't know what she'd said or done at the bar, but she knew that she needed to apologize to both of them, in person, and that meant getting her butt in gear.

Lindy dressed for the warm June morning in shorts and a tank and then headed out the door. Lonestar's, the only restaurant in town, had a bakery counter that sold amazing cinnamon rolls and other mouth-watering items. She waited in line, picking at the chipped polish on her nails, and ordered a box of cinnamon rolls and a box of blueberry muffins along with four cappuccinos.

Faith and McKenna shared a rental home on the other side of town from Lindy's own rental. When Lindy's mom had decided to leave the Tressel Pack to follow a male she met at a bar, Lindy had moved in with Faith and McKenna. Lindy wasn't sure if McKenna and Drake were going to get their own place or if Faith was going to move out. Lindy had been living by herself for only about six months, after deciding that she'd spent long enough not having her own place.

She parked in front of the home that her friends shared, and turned off the car. Gathering her purchases, she got out of the car and headed up to the front door. She kicked the door a few times, wincing as she stubbed her toes, holding two boxes in one hand and the cup carrier in the other.

After several minutes, the door opened, and Faith squinted at her in the sunlight.

"I come bearing a peace offering and many, many apologies, proverbial tail tucked between my legs and everything."

Faith tilted her head to the side and gave her a narrow look and then said, "I smell blueberries."

"And an apology?" Lindy asked hopefully.

"What does an apology smell like?" Faith asked in confusion.

"I don't know. Something bitter at first that gets sweet at the end?"

Faith smiled and opened the door wide. "I forgive you, you big bitch. Mac and Drake are still asleep. I'm tired as hell; those two went at it all night."

The door shut, and Lindy handed off the boxes. "Guess the walls aren't as thick as we thought originally."

"Not even close." Faith smirked and carried the boxes into the kitchen.

Lindy extracted a cappuccino from the carrier and took a sip as Faith opened the box of muffins she had set on the kitchen table. "You can move into my place," Lindy offered.

"Thanks, but I think I'm ready to get my own place. You had the right idea to move out on your own. I haven't ever lived by myself. I think I'd like to do that."

Lindy put the cup down on the table and took a deep breath. "About last night. I don't remember what I said because there's this big hole in my memory, but I know that I feel like shit because I hurt you and Mac and I'm so sorry. You're my best friends, and I don't know what I'd do without you guys."

Tears blurred her vision, and she tried not to cry, but she couldn't help it. "Oh, babe," Faith cooed softly, pulling Lindy into a hug, "I shouldn't have been such a bitch to you when you called. I was just pissed because Mac was upset and Drake was ranting about not just you but me, and…it was just a bad night all around." Lowering her voice slightly, she said, "I'm jealous, too."

"Really?"

"Yeah. You just said out loud what I was feeling. Mac never showed any interest in settling down, and one damsel-in-distress rescue from Drake and suddenly she's all about mating."

Lindy nodded, tearing a small piece of muffin off and popping it into her mouth. "She never went after the males like we did."

Lindy and Faith had systematically worked their way through every unmated male in the pack trying to find a mate. After a while they became the pack jokes, the *toys* that no male would actually date but many of them would fuck. The last-chance for a fuck when all the other options were gone.

Lindy related how she'd woken up with Bruce that morning, and Faith stared at her in shock. "I didn't know you'd sleep with him!"

Shaking her head, Lindy tried to ignore the memory. "I guess I was upset enough to say yes. I'm kind of glad I don't remember it. And I'm really fucking glad he used a condom! Can you imagine if I had gotten pregnant with his pup?"

Faith choked on her muffin, and Lindy whacked her on the back a few times. Gripping her hand tightly, Faith looked at her sincerely and said, "I promise I will never let you go home with Bruce again, no matter how pissed off we get at each other. Promise the same for me."

"Swear on my hair," Lindy said, using the vow they had used as kids.

"Why are you swearing on your hair?" Mac asked as she and a half-dressed Drake came into the kitchen.

Lindy related the story, and Mac made a face. "Shit, Linds, I'm sorry."

Drake snarled. "She insulted you, McKenna. Why are you sorry?"

"Because we're best friends, Drake. Friends don't let friends fuck assholes, and Bruce is the biggest one in the pack."

Mac stepped away from Drake, and Lindy hugged her, apologizing again and letting the tears loose once more.

Mac cupped her face and said, "I'm sorry that things turned out the way they did, Linds, but you'll find your knight in shining armor the way I did."

Lindy snorted. "I don't want to get groped in a parking lot by an asshole so a guy can rescue me."

"Worked for me." Mac winked, hugged Lindy again, and stepped over to the box on the table. "Oh, cinnamon. You're definitely forgiven."

"Even you, Drake?" Lindy asked. "I am sorry that I wasn't happy like I should have been."

The young male looked at her with eyes that showed a lot more wisdom than she had expected. "You're my mate's best friend, Lindy. If she forgives you, then I forgive you. But if you make her cry again, then I'm going to make you cry. Understand?"

Faith said, "Oh, I just got shivers. That was fucking cool."

"I promise," Lindy said, and she meant it.

Lindy didn't have the luxury of having a ton of friends or being well liked. She had caused a lot of trouble over the years for pack members with her behavior. She was a virtual pariah.

Drake swiped a cinnamon roll and went to take a shower, leaving the girls to talk. McKenna picked up a second roll. "I know I surprised you guys with my mating. Truthfully, I wasn't sure if he was sincere even though my wolf really liked him. My grandparents love him, and I think they knew there was something between us before we did."

Faith said, "You denied liking him for a long time."

She shrugged. "He's young. At first I told him that he was just infatuated with me because he didn't know any better. He wasn't entirely innocent, you know, but he's got a very naive outlook on life. He honestly believes that if you're mates then you just get together because it's the right thing to do. I was the one with the issues, saying he was too young, too inexperienced, afraid he would leave me if I let my guard down."

"What made you change your mind? Was it just him rescuing you at the bar?" Lindy asked.

"Not totally. I had to see him at the guard gate every time I visited my grandparents in the retirement community, and he was slowly wearing me down. But when he fought that drunk human who tried to rough me up in the parking lot, and I thought he might get hurt, I knew I didn't want to waste any more time. I mean, he fought for me. He was willing to risk getting hurt before we were even officially mates, and that meant a lot." Her brown eyes sparkled with tears. "You know, there were males in the pack who told him I was trash. That I wasn't worth more than a fuck or two before settling down with a proper mate. Gram said I shouldn't worry about what anyone else said, but it hurt that his friends tried to talk him out of mating with me."

"He didn't listen, though," Faith pointed out.

"Yeah, but it's scary to think that he might have listened. I didn't want to believe we were mates regardless of what I was feeling, and if he had just left me alone, then I wouldn't have fought it. I might have spent the rest of my life alone if he'd listened to them."

After some much-needed girl talk and reconciliation, Lindy left their home and went back to her own house to enjoy the rest of her day off. She didn't work weekends at Books & Beans, the bookstore and coffee shop where she had been working since she graduated from high school. Stella, the owner, had taken Lindy on even though she had no experience and hadn't read anything other than fashion magazines in high school. Stella made her read at least one new book a week as part of her job so she could make recommendations to people who came in to shop. After six years, and a few hundred books later, she really loved reading and talking to people about books and even lead a weekly children's story hour on Friday mornings.

But it was easier in Grawly, where no one knew her name or her reputation for being a pack whore. There, she was simply Melinda Vincent and nothing more. And that was okay with her.

Chapter Two

The following Thursday night was the full moon, and Lindy and Faith stood in front of the pack in the full moon meeting place, watching as Jason and Cades presided over McKenna and Drake's official mating.

As Jason unwound the mating strap from their joined hands, Lindy and Faith led the pack in cheering and howling in happiness for their friend. Lindy hugged McKenna tightly.

"I'm so happy for you, babe," Lindy said.

"Swear on your hair?" McKenna rubbed at the tears on her cheeks.

"Definitely."

"I'm going to miss hunting with you," Faith said as she stepped in to hug Mac.

Drake sidled close and pulled Mac against him. "Sorry, ladies, she's mine on the full moon."

"Just on the full moon?" She batted her eyelashes at him.

"All the time," he said with a growl.

Smiling, Lindy and Faith both rolled their eyes as Drake and Mac began to kiss.

"I got drafted to be a guard for the mates," Faith said. "Wanna go to lunch tomorrow?"

"I'm supposed to work. I'll drop by with takeout for dinner, though. Okay?"

"You bet." Faith left Lindy, walked over to where Cades and the other mates were waiting, stripped from her clothes, and began to shift. Each full moon, several wolves were chosen as guards for the mates that couldn't go hunting. Aside from Cades, who was a hybrid and unable to shift, Jenna, Reika, Karly, and Shyne didn't shift either. Shyne was human, Jenna was fae, Karly was an angel mate, and Reika was pregnant.

Looking around the clearing, Lindy knew she needed to find someone to hunt with. For the last few months, someone had been leaving traps around the pack's hunting territory. No one had been able to figure out who was leaving the traps, so Jason had declared that all wolves had to go out in groups of two or more to ensure that if someone did get hurt, there was another who could get help. She, Faith, and Mac had been hunting together since they were teenagers. It was strange for her not to have her friends with her.

For a moment, she almost asked Cades if she could stand as a guard so that she and Faith could go hunting together later, but the mates and guards were already on their way back to the house.

Spying Luka, one of Drake's friends, pulling his shirt off near some other males she said, "Hey, Luka, can I talk to you for a minute?"

Luka was cute and lightly muscled, with pale skin and a dimple in one cheek when he smiled. He gave her a funny look and then walked over, his shirt held loosely in his hand. Taking a breath, she decided to put herself out on a limb.

"Want to hunt with me? I need a partner."

A small part of her hoped he would say yes, but the larger part of her expected him to say no. What she hadn't expected was for him to laugh loudly.

"Are you kidding me? Why would I want to hunt with the pack bicycle?"

"Pack bicycle? What are you talking about?"

He chortled louder. "You're the pack bicycle. Everyone's had a turn." He gave her a condescending pat on the head and said, "Tell you what, *bike*, if I feel like getting sucked off later, and no one better is around, I'll text you."

All the blood drained from her face for a heartbeat before shame made her cheeks flame. Her eyes filled with tears, as he began to laugh, and she ran blindly away from him.

She almost plowed right into a young blonde named Sunny. "Oh, shit, sorry." Lindy rubbed at her eyes and tried to get her emotions under control. She'd never been so humiliated.

"It's okay. Are you all right?" Sunny asked.

"Yeah." Lindy sniffled and straightened her spine. She would just go home and shift and run around in her backyard. She only needed a full moon hunting partner if she was going to be in pack territory. If anyone asked her why she'd headed home, she'd just say she was overly tired and didn't want to have to drive home after the hunt.

"Are you, um, going out to hunt?" Before Lindy could answer, she continued, "My parents told me to go out with my brother, but he ditched me for his friends. My parents thought that he was going to hunt with me, so they went out on their own and I can't find them. I don't want to get in trouble. Alpha Jason said we couldn't hunt alone."

Compassion washed through Lindy. She'd been young and innocent like Sunny once, but it seemed like a lifetime ago. Before she'd followed her mother's example and started having sex with any male who would look her way.

"I'd be happy to go out hunting with you."

"Yeah?" She brightened considerably, flashing a wide smile. "Thanks!"

Lindy and Sunny stripped and shifted into their wolf forms. Lindy shook herself out from head to tail, flexing her claws in the dirt. Sunny seemed to be waiting for her to take the lead. With a short bark, Lindy loped away from the clearing, and Sunny stayed right by her side as they moved into the woods and began to hunt.

Lindy loved to hunt in her wolf form. There was something very freeing about just letting go of her human troubles and giving herself over to the wolf instincts. Natural wolves had it easy. Hunting, fucking, taking care of pups. The wolf shifters were the ones who had it hard, having to find a balance between the wolfish instincts that wanted to *only* do those things and the more practical human side that knew those couldn't be the only things in life.

Lindy's instincts took over, and the last of her human thoughts slid away as she scented a deer and took off toward it. Sunny stayed by her side the whole way, catching sight of the doe at the same time that Lindy did. The doe took off as they closed in on it, and they chased after her, bounding over fallen trees, brush, and a small, winding creek that crisscrossed through the territory. Lindy leapt at the doe and caught her flank with her paws, making her lose her footing and roll to the ground. She and Sunny fell on her, and Lindy snapped the doe's neck quickly to end her life and then lifted her head to the sky and howled, rejoicing in the kill.

After they had feasted, they left the remains of the kill to some other young wolves around Sunny's age and headed back toward the full moon meeting place. Lindy had enjoyed hunting with Sunny. The girl had let Lindy lead, and being in charge had brought a sense of satisfaction to Lindy that she hadn't felt in a long time.

When they reached their clothes, they both shifted back to their human forms. It was then, as she looked down at her clothes on the ground, that her satisfaction waned. Short-shorts, crop top, high-heeled sandals. Luka had called her the pack bicycle. She certainly dressed the part.

"Something wrong, Lindy?" Sunny asked as she tugged a very feminine sundress over her head. Lindy would not have been caught dead in something so innocent looking before this moment, sure that it would have been met with questions about her sanity for abandoning her normally revealing clothing.

Revealing? She snorted inwardly. Try slutty. Hooker chic.

Tugging the shorts and top on quickly, she picked the sandals up by the straps and then looked at Sunny. "Are you happy?"

Sunny paused in braiding her long hair. "I guess so. I just graduated at the top of my class, my dad said I could have his car to drive to college in the fall, and I just found out my mom got me a plane ticket to visit my favorite aunt in New York for two weeks in August. Why? Aren't you?"

"I thought I was."

Sunny cocked her head to the side as she finished tying her braid and flung it over her shoulder. "My gram says if you're not happy then you have to get busy getting there."

She smiled. "Sounds like a pretty smart lady."

"She was," Sunny said, beaming. Two adults that Lindy recognized as Sunny's parents appeared.

"Hey, Sun, you ready to go?" her mom called.

"Sure. You need a ride home, Lindy?"

"Thanks, but I drove."

Sunny's father put his arm around her shoulders and looked at Lindy. "Thanks for watching out for our girl."

She was about to answer when Sunny's brother, Paul, one of Luka's friends, strode into the clearing. "Tell me you didn't let her go hunting with that *female*?" Paul blocked Lindy's view of the family as he spoke. His voice was low, but she still heard every hissed word.

"You planning on letting Sunny whore for the pack?" Paul snarled.

"No!" his father answered in shock. "What are you talking about?"

Paul's voice slipped deeper, angrier. "You're letting my little sister hang out with the biggest slut in the pack. What do you think will happen?"

Lindy's heart fell into her stomach, and her face burned hot with blush. Sunny's dad straightened and gave Lindy a withering look.

"Stay away from our daughter."

Lindy's mouth fell open. Paul gave her a dirty look that slid into a sneer as Sunny's parents pulled her with them through the woods, speaking in angry, hushed tones. Sunny looked over her shoulder at Lindy and mouthed, *I'm sorry.*

Lindy nodded as tears filled her eyes once more.

Not wanting to run into them in front of the alpha's house where everyone had parked, she walked the long way around, got into her car, and drove home, devastated beyond compare.

Chapter Three

Fae Realm, Winnower Glen

Crimson Ta'rek collapsed against a thick tree and only kept hold of his sword by sheer force of will. The *rukh* cawed loudly, circling overhead. The large beast had descended from its home in the mountainous region of the glen and began attacking the fae who called the glen home. The fae ruling council had called in the military, and Crimson was asked to lead a small army to either kill the beast or drive him back up to his nest.

The bird was not going willingly, however. Crimson's army had been reduced by half at least, as the bird tore trees from the ground with its beak and used them like clubs to take out his men. The beast had dropped boulders on his people, squashing them flat with sickening thuds.

He took a few deep breaths and listened for the beast's location. He counted the survivors and found only six of his original thirteen. His inner beast roared at the loss. Thirteen fae warriors should have been more than enough to drive the beast back up the mountains or kill it, but the creature seemed hell-bent on destroying all of them.

Sheathing his sword between his wings, he motioned to his fellow men that he was going to try to spell the creature and asked for their help. Crimson was a *wulfen*, and therefore both fae and wolf. He was a physically strong fae, with feathered wings that allowed him to fly. He could also shift into a pure white wolf.

His best friend, Riyad, darted between trees and pressed his back against the same tree. "You need me?"

"Yeah." He looked around the tree and saw that the creature was circling over the homes, shrieking loudly and swooping down to snap and claw at them. "See if you can send up some vines to grab hold of his legs. When he's tethered, I'm going to fly up behind him and try to put a sleep spell on him."

"If he falls asleep over the homes, he'll smash them all when he falls to the ground."

Crimson rolled his eyes. "Then pull him away from the homes with the vines, Ri."

Riyad clicked his tongue. "Gotcha."

Crimson shook his head and concentrated on the spell he was going to cast. He could control fire, but he didn't think the beast deserved to be fried to a crisp. If this didn't work, however, he'd have to consider it.

Riyad began to speak his spell, and Crimson felt the trees stirring around him as his friend reached into the earth and called for vines to spring up and trap the creature. He shifted to look around the tree and watched as dozens of vines shot upward into the sky, wrapping around the beast's clawed feet. It squawked in alarm and tried to snap the vines from its legs, but there were too many of them. Riyad slowly pulled the creature away from the homes.

Nodding at his friend, Crimson shot up into the air and circled high around the enormous bird. It struggled to untangle itself from the vines, but Riyad continued to send more up to keep him held tightly. Folding his wings down along his back, Crimson raced through the air and landed on the bird's back, snagging a feather in his hand. The feathers were bigger than he was, and his fist barely closed around one of them. The bird went wild, screaming in fear as it felt Crimson's weight along its back. He held on and began to speak the spell to send it to sleep. It worked quickly, and the bird succumbed to the spell and began to plummet downward. It hit the ground with a dull thud.

He straightened and flapped his wings a few times, settling down onto the ground as Riyad and his men came out of the woods with a cheer. Bront knelt down next to the bird's legs and said, "Good work with the vines, Riyad."

Riyad practically preened. "Thanks."

"What's this?" Bront asked. Crimson knelt next to him and looked at what appeared to be a feathered dart protruding from the meat of the bird's leg.

He pulled it free and sniffed the pointed end. He let out a harsh breath. Bront waved his hand in front of his face with a grimace. "I can smell the *feltawin* from here! Someone put a dart in this bird with a tincture meant to drive it insane? What the hades for?"

Crimson stood up and looked at the homes that were in shambles and then at the sleeping bird. "I don't know, but I'm damn well going to find out."

Crimson paced outside of his father's study. He had just come from the formal inquiry into the *rukh's* rampage. It had taken less than a day for the authorities to find the maker of the tincture that had turned the normally calm bird into a raving beast that had killed over forty fairies, including seven of his men. The farmer, who lived in Winnower, had inadvertently created the insanity-inducing tincture while trying to concoct a drug that would kill the bird. It had carried off several of his livestock, and he was angry at the loss. Unfortunately, the man had been severely injured during the bird's rampage and had since passed on into the great beyond.

His father called from behind the closed door. "Come in, Crimson, before you wear a hole in my floor."

Crimson straightened his formal military jacket and opened the gilded double doors, striding inside the study. His father sat behind a desk carved from a large piece of gold-veined marble. As a child, Crimson had played under that desk while his father, who had attained the rank of general in the military, had mapped out strategies.

"How was the inquiry?" his father asked. Although retired, his father still bore the twin braids at his temples that marked him as a warrior for their people.

Crimson settled into the straight-backed chair across from the desk and let out a sigh. "The council ruled to break up the farmer's belongings and sell them, using the money to make repairs to the town."

He arched his brow. "You're not satisfied?"

"Of course not. Over forty fae died because he was upset a bird took a few of his cattle. And he had the nerve to die before he could be punished!"

His father chuckled. "I understand your frustration, but the important thing is that the bird was taken back to its nest and the glen will be repaired."

Crimson ran a hand through his short hair and sighed. He chose not to grow his hair long and braid the sides like most of the warriors did. He had never cared for long hair, finding it cumbersome and a hassle. "You wanted to see me?"

"I understand that you turned Giwyn from your bed last night." His father rested his arms on top of the desk and folded his hands.

Crimson tensed. When he'd returned from the battle, he'd spent hours going to the homes of the families of the men that had perished with the rampage, sharing the news of their deaths. As captain, the task had fallen on his shoulders. When he arrived back at his home within the Homelna Glen, the only thing he wanted to do was clean the blood and dirt from his skin and fall into bed for about a week. As he'd walked from the bathing room into his bedroom, he'd been utterly surprised to find a naked woman stretched out on top of his bed.

She had blinked dark eyes at him and cupped her tiny breasts, spreading her legs in invitation. She clearly assumed he would be happy to find her naked and willing, but all he was at that moment was supremely pissed off. Finding her clothes on the floor, he'd tossed them at her and barked at her to get dressed. At first she looked hurt, as if he'd wounded her with a blade, but then she looked angry. Dressing, she stormed through the house and declared that he would be sorry that he turned her down. He hadn't cared enough to even learn her name. Which was apparently Giwyn.

"Mother cannot keep sending females to my house, Father. The one before this one wouldn't leave, and I had to trick her to get her out of my bed."

His father shook his head. "When I was a young male, burying my cock into willing female flesh was considered a good time."

He snorted, refusing to allow thoughts of his father plowing *willing female flesh* to take root in his brain. "I don't want the sort of females she keeps sending to me. They're thin as rails, stuck up, and only interested in me because of my status in the military."

"So you'd prefer a chubby fae for your bride, then?" His father chuckled.

Crimson stifled a growl. The beast part of him didn't appreciate the random females that kept showing up. His wolf wanted to find its mate, and each full moon that passed made him more irritable.

"I don't care what my bride is. Don't you think that if my female were a fae that I would have found her by now? I've been all over the realm with the military. My beast is driving me insane. He doesn't want anyone but his mate, and I'll be damned if I can find her." He'd long ago lost the urge to just find a random female and have fun for a few hours. The shallowness of random sex had definitely lost its appeal.

His father hummed. "You're twenty-six, Crimson. You should have mated in your twenty-fifth year. It reflects poorly on your mother that you haven't taken a bride yet." He paused and settled the weight of his dark eyes on Crimson. "If you won't mate one of the females that your mother has sent to you, then you know what you have to do."

He'd been so busy striving to live up to his father's awe-inspiring reputation in the military that he hadn't really focused on mating. He'd always had one more battle he wanted to win, one more rank to attain. But if he didn't do something, then his mother was going to continue to send females to him or, worse…she might try to force him into an arranged marriage. Mothers less insistent than his had succeeded in trapping their sons into marriages they had arranged. Judging by the females his mother kept sending to him, she was hoping he would mate with a highbred female so she would be elevated in status as well. She meant well enough, he was sure, but she was hoping for the best for herself, too.

Nodding, he said, "I need to spell for my truemate."

His father nodded. "You have no choice. Your mother will continue to try to find a suitable bride for you, the same way that my mother did. However, I was lucky enough to find my mate within the first few months of her interference."

"The practice of the mother choosing the bride for her son is ridiculous. How can she possibly know what I want in a female?"

He smiled. "She doesn't, and that's why you have to take the choice away from her. If you don't spell for your truemate, then I'm afraid she may go so far as to try to force you into a mating. I would stop her if I could, but you know how determined your mother can be."

Nodding, Crimson stood up. "I'll do it on the next full moon."

"I wish you luck in finding your mate, son."

Crimson closed the doors behind him and hurried to his home. If he was going to spell for his truemate, then he had several things to get done first, the least of which was getting his house cleaned and finding a way to get his mother off his back while he made his plans to find his mate.

Chapter Four

The day after the full moon, Lindy went to work, plastering a smile on her face and chatting brightly with customers. She might look as though she was having a good day, but inside she was a wreck. She hadn't slept well once she got home after the full moon hunt. The insults she had suffered had lobbed around in her brain like tennis balls. It wasn't as if she didn't know she had a reputation within the pack. She had made the choice as a teenager to give in to her desires and have sex whenever she felt like it. It hadn't been hard, when she was younger, to find a male who was interested. As the years went by, the available males abandoned her and found mates, making it clear that she wasn't a worthy choice. When that happened, she hadn't changed her ways; she had simply tried harder to seduce the single males.

She'd hidden her lack of arousal under heavy perfume as she tried to find a male who would find her worthy of being a mate. But no one wanted her. The males in the pack began to find their truemates, and Lindy became a joke, a female that could be visited in the dark of night to slake a need but never taken out on a date, never taken to meet the male's family or friends. She had honestly believed that eventually a male would find her worthy of more than a late-night fuck, but after Luka's insult and the way Paul's family had ordered her to stay away from Sunny, as if she might be tainted in some way, Lindy was beginning to believe it was impossible.

When she got home, she called Faith. "I'm just feeling like staying in tonight."

"What's wrong?" Faith demanded.

Lindy hadn't told anyone what had happened on the full moon, but she didn't keep secrets from her friends and had no intention of starting now. Within minutes, she'd told Faith everything that had happened.

Faith growled. "I'm so pissed! Those assholes! Sunny would be lucky to have a sweet, protective friend like you. And Luka, I could cut off his balls and feed them to him!"

Lindy smiled as she wiped away the tears that had fallen while she shared her heartache. She had tried not to let the night's events hurt her feelings, but she'd been wounded deeply.

"Maybe my mom had the right idea about starting over. Maybe I should just pack up and move to her place and start fresh."

"Fuck. That. I'll be over in fifteen minutes to pick you up. We're going out."

"I really don't want to, Faith."

"Don't care. I'll be there." The call ended, and Lindy looked at the phone for a moment then put it on the coffee table. Walking back to her bedroom, she looked inside the closet. Tight dresses, micro-mini skirts, and revealing tops filled the walk-in. Her work clothes were relegated to a small section of the closet, but the remainder was filled with the sort of clothes that made men think with their dick and not their brain. Even her bedroom was a study in seduction, with satin sheets and a fur comforter, red light bulbs in the lamps, and a decorative bowl on the nightstand full of condoms. She'd prided herself on always being prepared, but all the bowl represented to her at the moment was the many males who'd visited her bed but never stayed.

Flipping through the clothes, she found a pale pink tank top with lace trim and grabbed a clean pair of jeans from the shelf where she kept her work clothes. Changing quickly, she applied only a little bit of foundation to hide the dark circles her nearly sleepless night had garnered her and pulled her long, blonde hair into a ponytail. She dropped to her knees and searched through her shoes until she found a pair of ballet flats, picked them up as she stood, and headed out of her bedroom.

Faith opened the front door without knocking, wearing a short, black dress and sky-high heels. "When I said 'go out'," she smiled, "I meant to a bar not a picnic."

Lindy sighed. "I'm trying something different."

Faith leaned against the wall and eyed her speculatively. "Different?"

"I'm tired of the trampy clothes. I hardly have anything decent to wear outside of my work shirts and jeans. If I ever did find a guy willing to mate with me, what the hell would I wear to meet his parents?"

Faith looked at her for a long moment and said, "When we talked about finding our mates the other day…are you trying to change yourself into a different person? Because it shouldn't matter what your clothes look like. A guy worth a damn is going to understand that."

"I know, but I'm miserable. I never thought that my life would turn out this way. When I planned my life at Sunny's age, I thought I'd be mated with a few pups by now. I have a lot of regrets."

"I do, too, but I'm not going to change who I am."

"I'm still the same person on the inside, but I kinda feel like this outside matches my insides better. Does that make sense?"

Faith snorted. "Are you saying my insides are slutty?"

"I'm talking about me. You said I looked like I was going to a picnic."

Faith rolled her eyes. "I was just teasing. You look pretty, and what's better is that you look happier, and that's important. You're not planning to go on some long search for your truemate, are you?"

"He's not in the Tressel Pack, that's for damn sure. I'll find him eventually. In the meantime, I want to figure myself out and get back to being happy all the time, not just with my clothes." She paused for a moment and said, "Remember when Jenna was attacked at the bar?"

Faith nodded. Lindy continued, "Logan came barreling out of the bar with rage in his eyes. He would have torn those wolves apart if they hadn't bugged out like cowards. Then he held her, and it was tender and loving. I want that."

Faith raised a brow. "Logan?"

Lindy rolled her eyes. "Of course not, he's mated. What I want is what they have together. That all-consuming passion that comes from finding your truemate. Knowing that you'd kill for your mate and that they'd kill for you, too. I want that. I want a male to love me enough to fight for me, to find me if I'm lost or hurt, to be there for me no matter what." She leveled her eyes at her friend. "I'm not going to find that by drinking myself silly every weekend and going home with whichever lowlife happens to be hanging around Jake's at last call."

Jake's was the only bar in Allen and owned by the Tressel Pack. The pack hung out there, but so did humans. It had been Lindy and her friends' weekend stomping ground since they'd turned twenty-one.

"I hadn't thought of it like that. So let's go somewhere that the pack doesn't go."

"Like where?" Lindy asked, grabbing her ID and cash and stuffing them into her back pocket.

"We can try that country bar up in Derven. I think it's called Boots."

Lindy agreed and offered to drive. After Faith buckled in, she said, "Do you think your truemate might be a human?"

Lindy pulled out of her driveway and headed toward Derven. "Why not? Michael's mate is human. And Logan's mate is a fairy. My mate might be a wolf or he might not be, but I'm pretty sure that he's not sitting in a booth at Jake's."

Lindy was happy that Faith had accepted her changes. Although it was small for now—she was really just wearing less revealing clothes—she felt different on the inside. It had hurt like a bitch when she'd been humiliated by Luka and then Paul, but she was beginning to think it was the best thing that had ever happened to her. She was only twenty-six. She still had time to change the course of her life and find her happiness. If she happened to find her mate in the process, well, that would be really sweet. But unlike how she'd felt for a long time, she didn't believe that her happiness lay with a male. She knew better now. Her happiness lay within her, and she was in control of it. No more hoping that a hot guy would notice her and say things that would make her feel good. That was hollow.

She glanced at herself in the rearview mirror after pulling into the parking lot of Boots and smiled. She looked younger than she did with her normal amount of makeup. Her eyes were very blue like a summer sky, and when she smiled, she had a small dimple in one cheek. Had she smiled for real recently? She didn't think so. But she was smiling now. It was a good start to the night.

Lindy pulled into the driveway and Faith kissed her cheek and hopped out, heading to her car that was parked in the street. Lindy watched her pull away from the curb and then got out of her car. It had been a long night. Lindy had offered to let Faith crash, but she wanted to go home and sleep in her own bed instead of on Lindy's lumpy couch.

As she closed her car door, she caught movement out of the corner of her eye and saw someone standing on her front porch. The porch light was on, but she couldn't see who it was because they were standing in the shadows. For a moment, she debated getting back into her car and driving away as she called the police. Crossing her fingers that she wouldn't regret her actions, she marched up the sidewalk.

"Who's there?" she demanded.

The figure chuckled and stepped into the light. But even without the light, she would have recognized Bruce by the sound of his laugh and the horrid cheap cologne that wafted off him the closer she got. She held back the disgusted sigh and looked up at him from where she stood on the sidewalk.

"What are you doing here, Bruce?"

He leaned against her front door and hooked his thumbs in his belt loops. He was mildly attractive, with blond hair and blue eyes and a muscular build. But his personality just sucked so much. He acted as if he were the best male specimen on two legs, and she knew quite well that his ego was largely inflated when it came to his prowess in bed.

"I thought you'd show up at Jake's tonight."

She didn't really like him leaning on her door. Or even being on her property. After their night together, she was determined that it would be their last one. She didn't want anything to do with him anymore.

"I went somewhere else." *Leave. Leave now.*

He raised his brows but didn't seem to actually care where she'd been. "You up for a quick tumble? I've gotta get up early for work."

Her mouth fell open. Had he really just thought she would show him in and drop her clothes because he'd decided to grace her with his presence? Judging by his expectant look, she had a feeling that he did indeed expect that.

"No thanks."

"Ah." He nodded. "On the rag?"

She closed her eyes as a headache began to form in the middle of her forehead. Rubbing the spot with her thumb, she said, "No. I'm just not interested in having sex with you tonight, or any other night." A little flare of anger rose up inside her. Just because she had behaved badly in the past didn't mean he, or any other male, had the right to treat her like the sex version of a 7-Eleven. She folded her arms and let her beast loose a little so that a growl rumbled from her throat. "You need to leave."

He snorted and shook his head, shoving off the door and striding past her. She watched him walk down the sidewalk. He paused and looked over his shoulder. "You've spread your legs for almost every unmated male in the pack, Lindy. I'm the only one that's still interested. You should think about that the next time I ask for sex."

She snarled and bared her teeth in displeasure. He laughed loudly and walked down the driveway. His car was parked across the street, and she waited until he was gone before she relaxed her aggressive stance and went into the house.

The following day at work, she re-shelved books and fumed over the situation from the night before. She and Faith had sat at a table at Boots and ordered drinks. The bar had been full of humans, and for once, she was glad to be in a place where no one knew her name or her past. It hadn't taken long for men to notice the two unattached women, and before long she was dancing the night away with different men and enjoying herself, the same as Faith.

As the night wore down, one guy, who had been paying close attention to her, asked her to come home with him. She thought he was handsome, but she wasn't looking for another one-nighter. She didn't want to be a notch on someone's bedpost or a booty call.

"How about I give you my number and we go out sometime?" she offered.

He gave her an incredulous look. "I'm not looking for anything but a good time. You in or not?"

In an instant, her good mood evaporated, and her self-esteem disappeared right along with it. Did she have *easy* stamped on her forehead or something? "Not," she said and turned to walk away.

His hand clamped on her upper arm, and he jerked her against his body with a scowl. "What are you, a tease? I bought you a drink."

She stomped her heel down on his foot, and he released her arm with a shout. "Bitch!"

"Go fuck yourself, asshole," she growled and elbowed him in the gut as she walked by. He cursed again, but she was too annoyed to care what he said about her, and she didn't really care anyway.

Faith left with her and put her arm around her at the car. "You'll find your prince charming, Linds, and it won't be some asshole who thinks a three-dollar soda is worth a blow job."

Lindy chuckled, but it was forced. She should have known better than to go to a bar looking to make a change to her life. She wouldn't find happiness sitting at a table in a dimly lit bar. At this point, she wasn't sure she'd ever find any happiness, but she was damn well going to try.

"Why do you look like you wish you were punching someone?" her boss asked, joining her in the YA aisle.

"Bad night."

Stella was in her late forties and didn't look like the sort of woman who normally owned a bookstore. Her arms were covered with tattoos, and she wore tight jeans, heeled boots, and heavy metal T-shirts. She was an amazing, sweet woman.

She was also very intuitive.

"If you're not happy with your life, Lindy, then make some changes. You're in charge of your happiness."

She hummed in her throat. She'd been thinking the same thing. "I don't like how I dress."

"Oh? I have some '80s rocker tees you might like." Stella smiled broadly.

"Thanks, but I mean the slutty stuff. It was…fun and freeing to wear that kind of stuff before, but now it just makes me feel like I'm displaying stuff no one wants anymore."

"So a new wardrobe, that's easy enough. What else?" Stella leaned against the shelf and listened while Lindy talked about redoing her home and purging the bad memories.

"You know something else you could do? Community service. You read to the kids once a week, which is awesome, but you could become more active in other ways, too. Have you considered that? You're talking about making outward changes, which is a good first step, but often helping others makes us aware of how good we have things and makes us feel better about ourselves, too."

Lindy put another book on the shelf and said, "I hadn't thought of that. I could start being more active in the pack and around town. Mac's grandma lives in the retirement community in Allen, and she would probably know about some people who might like a helping hand. Thanks, Stella."

"You're welcome, sweets. We've all been there, okay? I was a party girl at your age, too. Some women live that way their whole lives, never really settling down, moving from one adventure to the next. There's nothing wrong with that way of life, unless you are feeling like it's not for you anymore. You're allowed to make changes to your life, and if people don't accept what you're doing, then they can go to hell."

Helping people would take the focus off herself, get her out of her poor-me feelings, and give her a purpose. And if she could help with the pack, then she would feel more valuable as a pack member, and that was something she wanted now. *If* they were willing to accept the changes she wanted to make. She knew that Mac and Faith would accept her and love her no matter what, but she was unsure of the rest of the pack. And even if they didn't accept her, well, they could just fuck off.

Sunday afternoon, Cadence Gerrick put her daughter, Lyric, in the booster seat at the kitchen table and ruffled her blonde hair. "What's for lunch, little wolf? How about some delicious broccoli?"

Her nearly one-year-old daughter squealed happily and slapped her palms on the table a few times as she said one of the few words she could say clearly, "Chicken."

Cades grinned at her daughter. "You sound just like your daddy."

"Why, because she's so brilliant?" Jason asked as he strode into the kitchen. He snagged Cades around the waist and pulled her close.

"No, because she only wants meat. I can hardly get her to eat veggies." She sighed as Jason nuzzled under her ear.

"Meat's good," he growled, and the sound slipped down Cades' spine like a decadent caress. "You're better."

She slapped his shoulder. "Behave. Your daughter is hungry."

"When's her nap?" He nipped her neck and grinned.

"Soon, my feisty mate." He released her reluctantly and sat down at the table next to Lyric. Turning her attention to the refrigerator, she pulled out chicken breasts and put them on the counter. Cutting two breasts into chunks, she dropped them into a hot pan and gave them a stir with a long-handled wooden spoon. After cleaning up the mess she'd made, she poured a glass of apple juice and put it down in front of her daughter, asking Jason if he wanted anything for lunch.

He leaned back in the chair and hooked his arm over the back. She was momentarily frozen as she watched his shirt stretch over his muscular chest. He always had that affect on her. Made her brain fizzle out when he flashed her one of his panty-melting smiles or casually flexed. Although she doubted he did anything casually. He knew how much he affected her, and she was glad that she affected him the same way.

"I'm going to head back to the clearing. I'm thinking about widening the clearing by taking down some trees. Dad and Grandpa are meeting me back there."

"The pit could probably stand to be dug out again. Seems like we put less wood in it every full moon because it doesn't take much to fill it up. When we were kids, the pit seemed a lot deeper."

He gave her a smirk. "Maybe that was because we were smaller?"

She stuck her tongue out, and he laughed.

"I'll add it to the to-do list before the July full moon."

He stood and stretched, bending over to kiss Lyric on the cheek. "I'll be back, mate."

"I'll be waiting."

She watched him leave the house, enjoying the way his jeans hugged his butt. Turning her attention to lunch, she turned the chicken over in the pan and put together her own meal. Lyric was different than Cades, but that was to be expected. Cades was only half wolf, a hybrid with some wolfish abilities like fangs on the full moon and some extra sensory abilities, but Jason was a powerful alpha wolf. Lyric was not a full wolf, but she was showing wolf tendencies at an early age, which led everyone to speculate that she might be able to shift when she reached sixteen.

Cades wanted that for her daughter. She'd spent the better part of her life standing on the outskirts of the pack because she wasn't a true wolf. Sure she was alpha female, but she hadn't been included in pack dealings as a youngster and had grown up on the outside looking in. She didn't want that for Lyric. Or any other children that Cades and Jason had.

Dumping the contents of the pan onto a plastic plate decorated with Lyric's favorite cartoon character, Cades squeezed ketchup in a small dollop and added a few pieces of broccoli just for good measure.

"No, Mama." Lyric made a face, screwing up her mouth in a snarl that was almost exactly like Jason's as she pushed the broccoli off the plate and onto the table.

Cades chuckled, and put her own plate on the table, and had pulled her chair out, just as the doorbell rang.

Not wanting to leave Lyric alone, she called, "It's open!"

There was a pause, and then the door opened with a creak, closed, and footsteps came down the hall toward the kitchen. Cades' mouth fell open in surprise as Lindy stood in the archway of the kitchen. She looked…different. Her long, blonde hair was pulled back in a French braid, she wore almost no makeup, giving her a youthful, fresh-faced look, and she wore a pale peach T-shirt and tan capris with blue tennis shoes.

"Lindy?"

"Hi. I'm sorry to come without calling first, but I was hoping that you might have some time to talk?"

She glanced at Lyric, who had taken one look at Lindy then turned her attention to the plate of chicken. "Sure. Have a seat. Have you eaten?"

"I'm good, thanks." She pulled out a chair across from Cades and sat down.

Cades sniffed. "You smell like herbs."

Lindy blushed slightly. "That's sage. Faith and McKenna helped me smudge my house after we cleaned it yesterday."

Cades frowned. "Smudge?"

"You light a bundle of dried sage and use the smoke to cleanse the negativity out of your home. The scent is kind of everywhere in my house and on my skin still. Sorry if it bothers you."

Thoroughly intrigued, Cades pushed her plate aside. Lindy had cleansed the negativity from her home? Why?

Seeming to read Cades' mind, Lindy told Cades that she had taken a good, long look at her life and wasn't happy with what she had become.

"I know I've made a lot of mistakes," she said earnestly, "but I want to change. I'm tired of being a pariah, a joke." She glanced at

Lyric and then at Cades. "I'm just like my mom. I followed in her footsteps to the letter. Except she's never gotten tired of the endless males and trying to *bed* her way into a mating. I wish I could go back in time and tell my teenage-self that the road I was about to head down would lead to heartache and loneliness."

It was true that Cades had never cared for Lindy personally. They were the same age and had been in school together, and Lindy and other females like her had taken immeasurable joy in making sure that Cades knew she was different and not wanted. She'd gone after Jason, Michael, and every other unmated male in the pack. When Cades took over as alpha female, Lindy, along with the other females in the pack, had accepted her as their alpha. While the females who had picked on Cades as a youth had changed their tune, some of them, like Lindy, had simply focused their attentions on finding another male once Jason was claimed.

Cades could admit that she'd never really thought much about the females who weren't active in the pack. She spent time with her mother-in-law, Tina, the mates she was close to, and those few females who really wanted to be part of the pack.

"I didn't know you were feeling so lost, Lindy. I'm sorry that I haven't shown much of an interest in you and your friends. I just assumed you were happier to have little to do with the pack."

Lindy toyed with one of Lyric's stuffed animals that were strewn across the table. "I was happier, for a while. But I took a good look at myself in the light of day, and I hate what I saw. I don't want to be that girl anymore. I want to bury her and embrace the person I feel is the real me, the one I always kept muzzled."

Cades felt a genuine connection bloom between herself and Lindy. She was asking for help. Cades could be petty, but she didn't think that was the way an alpha should act.

Leaning back in her chair, she said, "It won't be easy. The pack won't accept that you've changed, not right away."

"I'm doing it for myself, not for anyone else. If they don't like the new me, that's okay, because I do." She rubbed the collar of her shirt. "I threw out all my trashy clothes and shoes. Faith helped me take everything to Goodwill. I redecorated my house and got rid of everything that reminded me of the person I used to be. I like to knit. I never told anyone that. I had a teacher in elementary school who showed me how one day when my mom forgot to pick me up from school. Last night I went to a craft store and got yarn and needles and started making a scarf." She smiled. "It felt really good."

Standing to refill Lyric's juice, Cades turned back to the table and said, "Good for you." Sitting down again, she said, "Tell me what I can do to help."

Lindy exhaled slowly and outlined a plan to help out around the retirement community. Cades offered her own suggestions for things she could do, including helping out more with the pack's full moon celebrations.

"Tell you what. Come back and see me in a couple weeks and let me know how things are going. If anyone gives you a hard time, let me know immediately, okay?"

"I will. Thanks, Cades."

"You're welcome." She stood as Lindy stood and was surprised when she came around the table and gave her a quick hug.

"I'm sorry for all the trouble I gave you when we were young," Lindy said. "You didn't deserve it. I was jealous of you and behaved in a petty and stupid way. Thank you for seeing past all that bad behavior. I was worried you'd send me away."

"The past can stay in the past where it belongs. I'm willing to move beyond it, if you are."

Lindy nodded and left.

"Well, wasn't that interesting?" Cades said to Lyric, who was rubbing her fingers in the leftover ketchup and painting a picture on the table.

"Mama?" Lyric licked her finger and then popped it back into the ketchup.

"Yeah, baby girl?"

"Chicken."

The following week, Lindy spent two hours after work every night helping out Mac's grandma, Eula. Eula was a very active senior who liked to take walks around the community and visit with everyone. Lindy accompanied her on the walks, carrying packages of baked goods or meals that Eula made. At first, the elder wolves had seemed wary of Lindy being around, and she'd worried that she wouldn't be accepted. But Eula was a firecracker and refused to allow anyone to treat Lindy badly. It didn't take long before she felt at home in the community.

Shyne, the mate of the second ranked in the pack, Michael, passed Lindy on Thursday evening as she made the rounds with Eula. "Hey, I was looking for you!" Shyne said. She was a pretty Latina with a bright smile.

"You were?"

"Yeah. Are you free on Saturday? Cades said you were willing to help out with pack stuff, and the retirement community is having a yard sale, and I could really use some help handing out flyers at the entrance to the community on Saturday."

"I'd love to."

"Great! Come to the community center at seven a.m., and we'll get ready for the crowds!"

Eula gave her a nudge with her elbow. "I told you that people would be able to look past your history if you just gave them a little time."

"It's a start," Lindy agreed.

Which was how she found herself helping pass out maps to the various yard sales within the community on Saturday morning. Shyne stood with her, and they passed out flyers to the humans and wolves who came through the gates. It was the first community-wide yard sale, and the proceeds were going to help build an addition onto the community center.

Although there were some pack members who looked at Lindy with barely veiled disgust, for the most part, she was treated like a member of the pack. And it felt damn good.

The next week passed quickly as she continued to walk around the community with Eula each night, and over the weekend, she helped out at Lonestar's where Karly, the mate of the third ranked male, Linus, ran things. Lindy had been surprised to get a call from Karly asking if she could help at the bakery counter on Saturday and Sunday, but she had been happy to do it. Standing with Mrs. B., who baked all the delicious things, was entertaining as the older woman regaled Lindy with tales of knights in shining armor that she read about in her many romance novels. Mrs. B. was a sweet woman with a rosy outlook on life that Lindy found infectious.

When Lindy stopped on Sunday evening to visit with Cades as she'd asked, her alpha was beaming with pride.

"I can't tell you how happy I am for you, Lindy," Cades said as she sat with her on a couch in the front room. "You look so happy."

"I *am* happy. I had no idea how much I'd enjoy helping others, but I really do. It's made me feel connected to the pack in a way I never felt before. I just feel bad for all the time I wasted."

"Don't. You can move forward now and you want to, and that's the important thing. So I have a request."

"Name it."

Cades laughed. "I like your enthusiasm. Jason said the males are complaining that none of the females are doing their fair share with the full moon clearing. Jason and some of the males cleared out another ring of trees to make the clearing bigger, so there's more that needs to be cleaned up. Do you think that you and Faith would be willing to help out this month?"

Faith had been doing her own version of cleaning up her life and had opted to enroll in community college to work on a nursing degree, something she'd wanted to do but had never pursued.

"Absolutely."

"Great! And I've never asked you before, but would you be willing to stand as a guard? I know you two like to hunt together, so you and Faith can both guard the mates and then go hunting afterward. I know Faith already guarded last month, but I hope she won't mind."

"I'm sure she won't. I'd be honored."

"Oh sure," Cades snorted and rolled her eyes, "it's very exciting sitting around babysitting all us women-folk while the men-folk all go out hunting."

"It's important. If I was pregnant and unable to shift, I'd want to make sure that the people watching over me were glad to be part of the guards."

"You think about having pups?" Cades asked, tilting her head in curiosity.

"I do. I think about finding my truemate and settling down and having pups. I don't know when that will happen, though."

"Your mate's not in the pack." She said it as a statement not a question.

"No. But we'll find each other when the time is right. I was in a hurry before, trying to force myself into a mating that wasn't right for me. Now, I just want to find the right person, and whenever it happens, it will be the right time."

"That's a really good attitude to have." Cades smiled, and Lindy nodded.

"Thanks for trusting me and for helping me. I don't deserve it, but I'm grateful for it."

"You deserve to be happy. I'm glad I could help."

With a skip in her step, she left her alphas' home and spent the rest of her day off helping Faith move into her own small rental home on the same street as Lindy's house.

The morning before the full moon, Lindy dressed in comfortable shorts, hiking boots, and a dark T-shirt she didn't mind getting dirty. When she was a teenager, she'd been part of the full moon cleaning crew, but she'd somehow managed to get out of the duty for the last few years. Maybe because Jason and his males always seemed to choose only males to work, or maybe because no one really wanted her around. Either way, she was excited to get her hands dirty.

Stopping to pick up Faith and then Mac, she headed to their alphas' house and parked on the grass. They walked through the backyard and into the woods to the clearing. Jason, Cades, and a handful of males stood around the firepit. Cades greeted them. "The guys are going to dig out the firepit so we need to work on clearing the debris. We'll bundle up the twigs to use as kindling, so those will go in the wheelbarrow over there where the ball of twine is. After we're done, Karly is bringing lunch to the house for us."

"Let's get cracking!" Mac said. "I'm starving already."

The four women worked, talking and laughing like old friends. It made Lindy proud that her alpha was so accepting of them and also that her friends were happy to be more active participants in the pack. Mac wielded a rake and picked up leaves while the other women gathered sticks and tied them into bundles.

While they worked, Mac told them about her overstuffed closet. Drake had officially moved in over the weekend and apparently had a penchant for shoes and clothes that she hadn't been fully aware of. Lindy laughed, and Mac threw a handful of leaves at her.

"It's not funny. I had no idea he was such a clothes hoarder. He's even got more shoes then me!"

And that was saying something. Mac's shoe collection was epic and often made Lindy green with envy. It was too bad they didn't wear the same size.

"Do you want some help organizing things?" Lindy asked.

"Yes, please." McKenna brightened considerably. "I'll leave the door open and you guys can come in and steal all his stuff, and I'll just feign ignorance."

Cades chuckled. "Leave the poor guy some pants!"

Mac snorted. "I'll think about it."

Linus' phone chirped, and he looked at it and said to the group, "Karly says lunch is ready."

"I'm starving," Lindy said, tying a bundle of twigs and carrying it to the wheelbarrow.

"Me, too," Cades said. "Thanks so much for helping. It's good for the females to take part in the full moon prep."

"I'm glad I could help." Lindy's back ached a little from all the bending and picking up, but a sense of satisfaction had settled over her as she worked, a rightness that she was exactly where she belonged. It might have been easier to leave town and start over somewhere else, but the only place that had ever felt like home to her was Allen.

And it was good to be home.

Chapter Five

Crimson stood outside his commander's office in the military training complex. He had spent the previous day cleaning his home after his chat with his father and had spent a good portion of the day thinking.

"Captain Ta'rek, you may enter," Commander Fenick said loudly.

Crimson opened the heavy wooden door and entered the office. Fenick was one of the most decorated males in the military, and Crimson respected him a great deal. Outside of his father, there was no one that Crimson looked up to more than Fenick. Fenick was seated behind a massive desk and gestured to one of the straight-backed chairs across from it. Clipping the end off a mulberry cigar and lighting it, Fenick blew a few smoke rings into the air and gave Crimson a long look.

"Did you plan to tell me what you wanted, Crimson, or are you just going to watch me smoke?"

"Sorry, sir." Crimson cleared his throat. "I'd like to request a leave of absence during the next full moon. I want to spell for my truemate, and I believe the best time to do that is on the full moon."

"Because of your wolf?" Fenick raised a brow. "You can't do it any other time than the full moon?"

Crimson shrugged slightly. "I just feel like the full moon is the best time to do it." He couldn't really explain the feeling, but something told him to wait, and his wolf, although anxious, was not grumbling at him quite so much.

"Well, I don't pretend to understand what you deal with having a beast hanging out in your brain, but I do know that when a male is ready to find his mate, instincts are best heeded." He leaned back in his chair and blew a plume of smoke straight up. "Do you want to step down?"

Crimson straightened farther in the chair. The military had a rule that mated males could step down from infantry service and take less dangerous positions, such as patrolling and training new recruits. It had been one of the things he'd thought about while he cleaned his home.

"I'm going to wait until I speak to my truemate, sir, before I make any job changes."

"Good, good." He rolled the tip of the cigar in a marble ashtray and said, "When you settle in with your female, let me know what you want to do. If you do decide to step down from the infantry, you'll be missed. You're one of the best."

"Thank you, sir."

Crimson left Fenick's office and walked slowly down the hall. He passed offices of high-ranking military officers. In between the doors were paintings of important members of the military who had retired from service. Many of the males he knew from his father's time, many he'd read about in history classes. All of them warriors. When he was young, he'd envisioned his own likeness in the hall, a testament to a lifelong dedication to the military.

But since he had decided to spell for his truemate, had finally given in to the angry rumbling of his wolf, he could admit that his desires were changing. The most important thing didn't seem to be living up to his father's legacy but finding his truemate, making her happy, ensuring her safety. His wolf grumbled in agreement. They hadn't even found their truemate yet, and already the beast was arguing with Crimson about keeping his job and putting himself in harm's way.

What had he joined the military for? To follow in his father's footsteps. To make him proud. If he quit now, what did that mean about his dedication as a male? His honor? His loyalty? His wolf grumbled again, and Crimson sighed. He'd never considered being anything but a soldier. What else could he do?

Deciding to think about it later, he continued down the hall, left the compound, and headed home. The full moon would be here before he knew it, and there was still much to be done.

Crimson manifested his sword and struck at the practice dummy as it flew toward him on an elaborate pulley system. Pivoting, he struck again and again, envisioning some large creature instead of the dummy. A meaty-fisted *bronyak* or a winged *flinglan*.

Merik lounged nearby with Riyad. They had put down their swords already and were waiting for Crimson to finish for the day. He was usually the last one in the military training compound, but ever since he had decided to spell for his truemate, he'd been too busy preparing for his truemate to continue with his training regiment.

His best friends weren't trying to talk him out of spelling for his truemate, but he could tell they were concerned about what the future would bring. They were worried because he wasn't a full fae, and his truemate could come from anywhere. His journey to find her and bring her home could take years. Both Riyad and Merik had recently turned twenty-five and would spell for their truemates when they were ready. Like he had been, they were not ready to stop their training to settle down.

Except Crimson *was* ready now. Only a week remained until the full moon, when he would spell for his truemate and cross through into the Mortal Realm to find her. He didn't know what lay on the other side of the portal, and he wanted to be prepared physically to do whatever was necessary to protect her.

Now that he had set his mind on finding his truemate, he wished that he'd done it earlier. Years ago. So that he and his truemate could have grown up together and not wasted any time.

"Aren't you tired yet?" Merik asked.

Riyad laughed. "He's trying to make sure he's all toned before he meets his truemate."

Crimson released the sword, and it disappeared as one of the young apprentices in the compound drew the dummy away with the pulley. Crimson waved at the young male saying, "I'm done for the night." The boy, barely ten, nodded and began to repair the holes that Crimson's sword had left behind.

His friends were teasing him, and he accepted their ribbing with a smile. "I'm not doing anything different." He stretched fully and tucked his wings into his back, cracking his neck. Sitting down on the floor next to his best friends, he took a drink from a wooden cup of water and let out a long sigh.

"No?" Merik raised a dark brow. "You've been in the military since you passed the tests at age seventeen, a full year before most males. You raced through the ranks until you attained captain. You work harder, train longer, fight more fiercely than any other male. But for the last three weeks, you've been entirely focused on preparing your home for your truemate."

Crimson raised a brow. "When you spell for your truemate, don't you plan to prepare for her?"

Merik gave a loud snort. "I'm not going to pretend I'm something I'm not to impress a female meant to be mine, Crim. Don't you think you should have left your home as-is so that she'd know what she's getting into?"

"Hey, I'm a clean male; I've just been busy since the last battle. Give me a little credit."

Merik chuckled, and Riyad said, "I'll be sure to pull her aside and tell her just how much of a slob you are."

Crimson's wolf didn't much care for Riyad doing any such thing, and Riyad stopped laughing immediately as Crimson snarled. "Whoa, sorry, man. I was just kidding. Shit, leash that dog."

"Wolf."

"Whatever." Riyad rolled his eyes, and Merik gave him a shoulder shove, telling him to stop antagonizing their friend who could shift into a big, huge wolf.

Merik stood and offered his hand to Crimson, who accepted the help as he stood. "I'm happy for you, Crim. Whoever your mate is, she's a lucky female."

"Aw, I'm gonna cry, this is so sweet." Riyad said as he made a face.

"You're gonna get your ass beat if you don't stop being such a smart ass," Merik said.

Crimson laughed as the two began to swing lazily at each other and steered clear of their fists as he gathered his things to head home. Each day that passed brought him closer to spelling for his truemate. Riyad and Merik were right in some ways that he had changed over the last few weeks. He'd been obsessed with living up to his father's legend to the exclusion of all else, even his own happiness. He'd been content, but he hadn't been truly happy. Something had been missing, and he'd tried to fill the emptiness with service and training, but it hadn't worked. There was something very freeing about his decision to spell for his truemate, and he was glad he wasn't waiting any longer.

Riyad looked at the leather bag that Crimson packed. "You sure this is a good idea?"

"Definitely," he answered, folding a shirt and tucking it inside. After almost a month of preparing to spell for his truemate, he had come to the conclusion that it was well past time for him to settle down and start a family. Yes, he enjoyed living alone, coming and going as he pleased, but he didn't enjoy it so much that he would not take the opportunity to find his truemate. Since he'd been thinking about finding his mate, the house had begun to feel empty, and, in spite of his friends, he found himself feeling lonely.

"What did you do to get your mother to back off while you're gone?" Riyad plopped down on the freshly made bed, and Crimson growled at him until he got up. No one was getting on that bed until he and his new mate came back to christen the room. And every other room in the house.

"I told her I was really busy with training exercises for the first few weeks of the month, and then yesterday I sent her to the spa for a week with a few of her pals and said it was an early birthday gift."

"She bought that?"

"I don't know if she really bought it or not, but she was too giddy with the thought of going to the spa to really question me." There was a good chance that when his mother got back from her trip to the spa, if he hadn't already returned with his mate, that she would try to cause trouble, but there was really nothing she could do once he spelled for his mate. The truemate bond was sacred.

Closing the bag, he looked around the room to make sure he hadn't forgotten anything he'd planned to take along. Satisfied, he walked with Riyad out into the main room. His dwelling, like most in the Homelna Glen, was made of the slate colored stones found in the mountains. He'd grown up in the Ulnait Glen, but when he'd turned eighteen, he moved away from his parents' home and into Homelna, which was where the army mainly called home. It was well known as a soldiers' glen, where retired and active members built their homes by hand with the help of their fellow warriors. The military compound was in the center of town, along with market stalls where food and goods were sold and a tavern where they gathered to tell war stories and drink.

He walked out into the backyard where lush *givenon* trees shaded the stone walkway that led to his private fae ring. "Keep an eye on the house for me, but don't even think about touching anything."

He gave Riyad a good, hard glare, and his friend chuckled and put up his hands in surrender. "I swear on my mother's favorite hen that I will not set foot in your house. But if you die on your quest to find your truemate, can I have your stuff?"

He slugged Riyad in the shoulder. "You should try being serious, Riyad. Maybe you'd find your own truemate."

Riyad gestured at himself. "And deny the female population of our realm the joy of my incredible body? That hardly seems fair."

He gave him a shove on the shoulder, and Riyad left with a wave and a loud laugh.

Kneeling down in front of the portal, he set his bag down next to him and closed his eyes, trying to calm his beast. With each day that drew them closer to the full moon, his beast had been practically clawing him from the inside to find her. He readied the portal so that when he spelled for his truemate he would be able to be taken wherever she might be. As a wulfen, he was more powerful in some ways than other fae, and with his truemate spell, he would be able to go very close to where she would actually be. Most fae, when they spelled, would be taken to the same realm but might not be anywhere near their mate and would have to search.

He didn't know why it was that way, but figured it was just nature's way of making sure the warriors of their people didn't spend ages trying to find their one perfect mate. Now that he was ready to find his mate, he certainly hoped she was ready for him.

He took in a breath to begin the spell but paused. It was entirely possible that the truemate spell would lead him to a fae within his own realm or one living in the Mortal Realm. Because he never felt connected to a female fae in his realm, he believed that his truemate was not within the Fae Realm, but it was possible that his truemate might be a fae. Some fae didn't care for *wulfen* like himself, believing them to be little more than their beasts. He was one of only two *wulfen* living in the Fae Realm. *Wulfen* were so rare they were revered as much as they were feared. His truemate could be any kind of shifter or even human and might be terrified of his shifted form or even his white wings. His wolf shift was much larger than the Mortal Realm's werewolves. Frowning deeply, he didn't know what he would do if his mate was afraid of him.

Shaking his head, he banished the dark thoughts. If she was afraid of him, then he would seduce her so thoroughly that she wouldn't care if he changed into a horn-toed *wollbeast*.

Preparing the portal, he began to spell for his truemate. He was shirtless and wearing leather trousers, his wings extended from his back like shields to increase his power. His beast rolled under his skin, howling in his mind. As he finished the spell, he felt a great urgency fill him. The portal began to shimmer, and the spell altered the portal to allow him to go straight to his mate. He felt himself begin to shift, and he struggled to contain his beast, but the wolf would not stay confined, and he was unable to stop the shift.

His wings receded into his back as his body morphed from fae to wolf. Before he had finished shifting completely, he was aware of a female's pain and terror, and he roared in anger. His mate! He knew the female in agony was his truemate. He lunged though the portal with fangs bared and claws extended, ready to protect his mate to the death.

Chapter Six

Lindy parked her car in front of Jason and Cades' home on the night of the full moon. Her wolf was practically prancing in her mind at the thought of the night to come. She couldn't believe how a few small changes, plus a really big attitude change, had made her feel.

Faith climbed out of the passenger side and looked at her reflection in the window, patting at her hair. "Oh, the humidity is going to make me look like a big old puff ball by the end of the night."

"You're still gorgeous," Lindy promised, chuckling at the forlorn expression on her friend's face. "I always wished I had curly hair."

Faith had beautiful red hair that was wavy most of the time, but curled when it was wet. Or extremely humid like it was that evening.

"I always wished I had straight hair like yours."

Linking their arms, they walked up the steps to the front porch and through the open door of their alphas' home. It was her first full moon since she'd made changes to her life, and she felt like a true member of the pack for the first time since she'd joined when she shifted at age sixteen.

The large kitchen was mostly empty, as many of the pack members were milling around outside where Jason and several other males manned grills and cooked steaks, burgers, and hotdogs. Cades was standing next to her daughter, Lyric, who was sitting in a booster seat at the kitchen table. Karly's son, Remy, sat in a chair next to Lyric.

Remy, only a few months older than Lyric, picked up his pieces of steak and put them on Lyric's plate. She squealed with joy and fisted the pieces, quickly shoving them into her mouth.

"Oh that's so freaking cute," Reika, one of the mates, said with a chuckle.

"Remy's going to waste away to nothing if he keeps giving Lyric all his food," Cades said, smiling.

"He eats like a horse, and he had three hamburgers before we came over here. I'll go get him another steak, though," Karly said, heading for the back door.

"And one for Lyric, too, I guess," Cades said. She looked at Lindy and Faith. "Hey! Are you hungry? There's plenty on the grill."

"Thanks," Lindy said, accepting Cades' welcoming hug. Shyne and Jenna said hello to them as well, and they headed out to the back deck to get something to eat. The pack got together before the full moon to cook out and visit. Lindy grabbed a plate and stood in line behind Karly, looking over the backyard and the wolves gathered there. The pack wasn't that large, around forty wolves that could shift, but the non-shifting mates and young children made it seem much larger than it was.

"Good to see you, Lindy," Jason said, placing a steak onto her plate.

"Thanks." And she meant it. She and her friends had never come to the before-the-hunt get-togethers. They'd always hung out at one of their homes beforehand, showing up just before the full moon to hunt with the pack. And even then, they'd stayed together in their trio, not really interacting with others.

Faith and Lindy stepped off the deck and down onto the grass. They spied Mac and Drake sitting at a picnic table with some of Drake's friends, the males who hadn't been kind to her before. Not that she hadn't deserved the slutty title, but they didn't need to be such assholes.

"Lindy! Over here!"

Lindy was surprised to see Sunny waving excitedly. Sunny was sitting with two younger females. Lindy looked at Faith, who shrugged. They walked over to the table, and Sunny said, "Sit down. These are my besties, Laura and Honor. They're human, but Alpha Jason said they could come for the cookout. They're going to hang out with the mates until I'm done hunting, and then we're going to have a slumber party."

Lindy introduced herself and Faith and sat down, looking around surreptitiously. Just a month earlier, Sunny's parents had told Lindy to steer clear of their daughter, and Paul had been instrumental in that.

"Don't worry," Sunny said, drawing Lindy's attention to her. "Alpha Cades told my parents that you were a really nice girl and that they were judging you too harshly. She said I'd be lucky to have a friend like you. And," she lowered her voice conspiratorially, "she read Paul the riot act for being such a dick."

Laura giggled. "He *is* a dick."

Honor elbowed Laura, who stopped laughing as Paul came up to the table. He looked down at Lindy. At first, she saw concern in his eyes, but then, slowly, his expression changed to one of acceptance. "I'm sorry for what I said. If you and Faith would like to hunt with Sunny tonight, I'd like to come along and keep an eye out for you all. If you don't mind the company."

Lindy looked at him in surprise. He was only twenty, and she'd always thought he was kind of immature, even if he was very cute, but he looked a lot older and wiser in that moment.

"Faith and I are guarding the mates tonight, otherwise I'd take you up on your offer. And thanks for apologizing. It wasn't necessary."

"Um, yeah it was," Sunny protested. "He was a dick."

Paul cuffed her lightly on the back of the head. "Stop cursing, or I'll tell mom."

"Next month, then?" Paul asked, and Lindy nodded.

Paul left, and Faith cleared her throat lightly. Lindy looked at her, chuckling at her friend's wide eyes. "That was totally weird," Faith said.

"He's afraid of Alpha Cades," Sunny said. "Mom and Dad are out of town, and when Cades came over to talk to him, she gave him the impression that she'd tell on him if he didn't stop being so rotten to you. I told Mom and Dad that I was old enough to make my own choices in friendships. There aren't any females my age that want to run with me, and Paul doesn't really like me tagging along with him. I think he's afraid that I'll end up mated to one of his friends." She made a face while her human friends laughed uncontrollably.

Lindy was an only child so she didn't know what it was like to have an older sibling watching out for her, and with her mom constantly bouncing from one lover to another in her quest to find her mate, Lindy had never had a father figure either, or a good female role model. But she wanted all of those things for her own pups—to be there for them whenever they needed her, their father by her side, and to have lots of pups so they were never alone.

Lindy and Faith mostly listened to the young girls chatter about the cute males in the pack while they ate. The girls reminded her of her own friendships with Faith and Mac, when they'd been young and excited about the future.

When the meal was over, she and Faith walked with Sunny to the full moon meeting place. Cades and Jason stood near the roaring bonfire and called for the pack to shift and hunt. Tina, Jason's mom, came over and said, "I'm going to help guard tonight. Do you mind if I hunt with you two later on?"

"Not at all," Lindy answered, dropping her shorts and T-shirt to the ground.

"Thanks. Usually, Peter guards with me so we can go hunting together afterwards, but Jason asked Peter to hunt with him tonight."

Lindy nodded. "We'd be happy to have you along."

As she shifted to her wolf form, she shook herself out and sat down on her haunches, waiting until the others had followed suit.

"It's times like this that I wish I could shift," Cades said with a wistful sigh. Lindy and the others followed Cades back to the house where Karly, Shyne, Reika, Jenna, and the kids were waiting.

Lindy spent the next few hours watching the woods from the back of the house while the others guarded different sections of the house. The mates were inside along with the children. When she finally heard the call of the males coming back, she barked to her fellow guards, excited to get to hunt while the moon was still overhead.

Once the males were back with their mates, Lindy, Faith, and Tina took off to hunt. They raced off in search of game to chase. Her wolf hadn't minded watching over the mates, but now she was happy to be free. They chased rabbits and birds and found a few deer. She raced with the two females, enjoying the freedom that came from running in her shifted form.

Faith barked sharply in alarm, and Lindy spotted a trap hidden under some leaves and twigs just ahead. She tried to turn, but her paws slipped on leaves, and she skidded toward the trap. With a sickening crack, the trap snapped down on her back leg, and she howled in pain.

Tina darted off immediately, howling in alarm, and Lindy struggled, trying to get on her feet and move back to the safety of her alphas' house. The trap was staked into the ground with a chain, so she didn't get far, and each time she moved, the trap bit into her leg, and she screamed in her mind at the pain.

Slumping to the ground as pain washed over her in hot waves, she felt her eyes roll back in her head as Faith shifted into her human form and tried to pry the trap apart.

"Shit, Lindy, shit! I can't! It's too strong! Stay with me. Lindy? Linds?" Faith screamed her name, but Lindy was beyond the pain, beyond answering, and sinking down into darkness.

Chapter Seven

Faith Radcliffe's fingers cut and bled as she tried in vain to pull the trap apart. Lindy had gone very still, and Faith worried that her friend was either passed out from shock or from blood loss. The fur on Lindy's leg glistened in the moonlight as blood welled from the wound and pooled around her on the ground. Tears fell from Faith's eyes as she gripped the iron trap in her hands and tried once more to open it.

"Help! Someone, please, help!" she screamed, praying that Tina would bring help quickly.

The hairs on the back of her neck prickled, and the air seemed to shimmer around her. What first looked like a ray of sunshine just feet from her and Lindy spread until a hole opened, and she swore she could see a house on the other side.

An enormous white wolf leapt through the hole, and Faith screamed in alarm. It was like nothing she'd ever seen. It was the size of a small horse, with long, deadly looking fangs and thick black claws. It sniffed the air and stared straight at her. Her body shook in fear as she sat frozen on the ground. It seemed to dismiss her with a chuff, turning its attention to Lindy. The great beast nuzzled her and made an almost gentle, purring sound in its throat, snarling when it scented down her body and found the trap.

The creature's body twitched and jerked, and within seconds, the wolf had transformed into a man with white-feathered wings sprouting from his back. He waved one hand over the trap as he whispered a few words, and it fell apart. Then he lifted Lindy into his arms.

"What is her name?" he asked gruffly, cradling her close to his bare chest.

It took a moment for Faith's mouth to work, but finally she was able to say, "Lindy."

He smiled down at the wolf in his arms. "Lindy." Faith had never heard a more reverently spoken word.

The man moved toward the hole in the air.

"Wait! Where are you going with my friend?"

He turned enough to look at her. "To take care of her."

Without another word, he stepped through the hole, and it disappeared as quickly as it had appeared. Faith rubbed her eyes and stared at the place where the hole had been.

The sound of rushing feet alerted her to her pack coming, and the reality of the situation finally sank in. Lindy was gone. And Faith didn't know where she'd been taken.

An hour later, Faith was still sitting at the spot where the hole had appeared, waiting for Logan and his fairy mate, Jenna, to come. The highest ranking members of the pack stood around her and Tina, who had brought her clothes from the full moon meeting place and knelt next to her, one arm around her for comfort. Flashlights helped illuminate the area.

Jason and his second, Michael, were discussing the trap with Linus and Bo, who were pack third and fourth. They were all furious that another trap had been found. Unlike the previous trap that had been right on the edge of the territory, this one had been at least a hundred yards inside.

"Was the trap baited with meat of any sort?" Linus asked, rubbing his knuckles across his jaw in thought.

Faith shook her head. She'd answered questions about the trap since they'd shown up.

"It was covered with leaves. I saw something metal glint in the moonlight and I barked to warn Lindy. She tried to turn away from it, but her paws slipped on the leaves, and she landed right on it."

Logan and Jenna came through the trees. Logan said, "Sorry for the delay. What happened?"

They all looked at Faith expectantly, and she told the story once more.

Logan looked down at Jenna. "Sounds like a portal to me. But I didn't know that your people had werewolves."

Jenna shook her head and walked toward the trap. "We don't."

The trap lay in several pieces like someone had taken a hammer to it. But Faith had seen the man break the trap with his hand. And with those wings, he looked like an angel. A really pissed-off, naked one.

Jenna closed her eyes and took in a deep breath. Her wings slid from her back, the loose tank top allowing them to slide free without tearing her shirt. The pale blue and silver transparent wings looked very different from the feathered ones the man had. Her eyes were bright like silver coins, and she stood slowly and turned toward where the portal had been.

"I don't know why, but a portal to my realm was opened here. Someone very powerful came here. Even without my wings, I could feel the remnants of his power. He used a spell to open the trap, and then he took her through the portal. What did you see when you looked through the portal?" Jenna looked down at Faith.

"A house. It was dark there like it is here, but there was a light over a door, and it looked like the house was made of black stone."

Jenna looked at Logan and said, "It was a *wulfen*."

Logan's brow arched. "I thought you said that you didn't know of any *wulfen* alive today."

She shrugged. "I don't. But the Fae Realm is enormous, and although it's ruled by one governing body, there are many different armies that protect the various glens. Only warrior fae have feathered wings, and the only fae that can shift into large, white wolves are *wulfen*."

Faith shivered. "Why did he take her? What's going to happen to Lindy?"

Jenna's wings slid back into her body, and her eyes dulled slightly. She moved to Logan, and he pulled her into his arms.

She said, "A *wulfen* is a highly skilled, powerful warrior for my people. I don't believe that he took her to hurt her. There's no reason for a fae to randomly come here and happen to stumble upon a wolf in distress. I think that he spelled for his truemate and found her."

Everyone went quiet.

Bo said, "You were really far away from Logan when you spelled for him, though. Why wouldn't the spell have brought you straight to him if that were the case?"

"Well, first I didn't travel through a portal on my own; I was kidnapped. And second, I heard that when *wulfen* spell for their truemates that their power is so great that they are able to pinpoint where their mate is and go straight there."

Faith said, "He was huge. I've never seen such a terrifying wolf in my life."

Jenna smiled softly. "I've only seen pictures of them. They're very rare among my people, but I have no doubt that he was frightening." She looked up at Logan. "Let's go home. The sun will be up soon, and I can portal-call my parents."

Turning her attention back to Faith, she said, "I'm going to ask my father to find out where this *wulfen* male is, and then Logan and I will go speak to him and find Lindy. Rest easy. She couldn't possibly be in better hands than those of her truemate."

Tina helped Faith to her feet and hugged her. "Come back to my house and have some coffee. The sun will be up soon."

Jenna nodded. "I'll call you as soon as I know anything."

Linus picked up the broken trap, and Jason said, "Bring that back to my house. Logan, take your mate home and then call me so you can be conferenced into the discussion. We've got to find out who is planting these traps and stop them before someone else gets hurt."

Faith was numb from head to toe with worry over Lindy. Jenna said not to worry, but until Faith could see for herself that Lindy was okay, she was just going to keep on worrying. Lindy and McKenna were like sisters to her.

Once back at Tina's home, Faith called McKenna, who came straight over with Drake and sat with her in Jason's parents' home, waiting to hear from Jenna.

It had been a very long, horrifying night, and it wasn't over yet.

Chapter Eight

*L*indy. His mate's name was Lindy.

After assuring the woman that he would take care of Lindy, he raced through the portal, sealing it behind him as he darted into his home. He tugged a thick blanket from the back of the sofa and laid her on it. Her wound was still bleeding. He called the lights to come on in the room, and the lanterns and candles blazed to life. Moving to the kitchen, he opened a temporary portal and called one of the military healers who lived nearby.

A bleary-eyed Viscount stumbled into view. "You bellowed, Crimson?"

"I found my truemate, and she's seriously injured."

Viscount's eyes widened, and he snapped to attention. "I'll be right there."

The connection broke, and Crimson grabbed a pair of trousers from his bedroom and tugged them on, picking up a towel from the bathroom and going to Lindy. He pressed the towel to the wound and settled his ear on her furry chest. Her heart was beating slowly, and her breathing was shallow. He didn't know if a werewolf from the Mortal Realm could actually die from blood loss, or if her accelerated healing would stop the wound before that happened. His heart clenched as worry settled over him. He'd just found her. He didn't know what would happen to him if she died.

The door burst open, and Viscount strode in, a leather satchel slung over his shoulder. Crimson was surprised when Riyad and Merik followed close behind.

"What are you doing here?" he asked the brothers.

Riyad jerked his head toward the healer. "He told us to come along. We were just on our way home from the tavern when he came rushing by like his ass was on fire."

Viscount said, "Hold him while I check her out."

Before he could blink, Riyad and Merik pinned him to the wall opposite the sofa, their bodies pressed against his and their hands gripping his shoulders. "What the fuck?"

Viscount looked over his shoulder. "I'm going to have to examine her and possibly hurt her so she can heal. I don't want you ripping my head off, Crimson. You're a *wulfen,* and this is your truemate. You have no idea how protective you're going to be."

The healer turned his attention back to Lindy and put his hands on her body. Everything in Crimson's world narrowed down to Viscount's hands on his mate. He growled and tensed his body, his claws springing free from his fingertips as his fangs descended.

"Hades, Crim," Riyad grunted, "calm the fuck down!"

Viscount pulled the bloody towel away from her leg and began to stretch the damaged leg out. Blood dripped onto the floor, and she whimpered in pain. Crimson roared. "Don't touch her! I'll kill you!"

"Keep a good hold on him," Viscount warned.

"If he kills me when he shifts, I'm going to haunt you forever, Visc," Merik snarled angrily.

"It's about to get worse," Viscount warned.

Crimson's shoulders were shoved hard against the stone wall, the rough material cutting his flesh.

"Calm down! He's helping her!" Merik said harshly.

Crimson struggled. He knew that Viscount was helping Lindy, but his beast didn't want anyone touching her, let alone hurting her. The sight of her blood on the floor, coupled with the sound of her pained whimpers, was driving him insane. His beast was rolling and twisting under his skin to protect her at any cost.

"Hurry up, Viscount!" Riyad yelled.

Rage colored his vision red as the healer put one hand on her hip and the other on the paw of her injured leg and jerked hard.

There was a snapping sound, and she whined in pain, her body twisting and writhing as she shifted from her wolf form to her human form. Still unconscious, she rolled to her back, her face ashen and her leg covered in blood.

Crimson felt his skin prickle as his fur sprouted. He fought not to shift, knowing he would hurt his friends, but the urge to protect her was almost overwhelming.

Viscount poured clear liquid from a bottle over her leg and cleaned it up with a cloth. The scent of antiseptic filled the room, and slowly his rage began to ease as he realized that her leg was now entirely healed.

His beast retreated some, and he relaxed with a sigh, his head slumping forward.

Before Merik and Riyad relaxed, Merik asked, "Are you *resh* now, Crimson? Can you control yourself and your beast?"

"He's good," Riyad said.

"I want to hear it from him. There are certain parts of my body that I'm fairly fond of, and I don't want him to suddenly shift and slash off the protruding parts."

Crimson swallowed thickly and shuddered violently as his beast settled finally. "The female population can rest easy. I'm not going to tear off your cock."

They relaxed and moved away from him. His body sagged slightly, but he was too determined to get to Lindy to take care of her, so he stumbled forward. Viscount tossed the cloth and bottle into his bag and stood up, moving to the other side of the sofa. Riyad and Merik joined him. He snorted inwardly as he knelt next to his mate and pulled another blanket from the back of the sofa to cover her body. As if the sofa would stop him or his beast if he wanted to tear them apart.

"She's okay?" He looked up at Viscount.

"Her leg wasn't going to heal in her wolf form; it was broken and bleeding too fast for her healing to stop it completely. If she'd stayed in her wolf form, she might have remained lame for the rest of her life. I pulled the leg straight to align the bones and the pain forced her to shift back into her human form. That shift sped up her natural healing, and her bone is now completely healed and her leg is fine."

Relief flooded him.

"Thank you for coming so quickly."

All three men nodded. Viscount said, "She'll probably sleep for a few hours. She will most likely be starving when she wakes up, so make sure she eats and drinks plenty. If she has any lingering pain, give me a call, and I'll drop off some medicinal herbs to help, but she should be fine."

He watched his friends walk out and close the door, and he slumped against the sofa, his head resting on Lindy's bare shoulder.

"Hades, Lindy," he took a few deep breaths and the scent of her calmed him, "let's not tempt fate again."

He pressed his lips to her cheek and got up, going into the bedroom. He pulled the covers back on the bed and willed several candles to light. Returning to the front room, he lifted her gently into his arms and carried her to the bed, laying her down and tossing the blanket from the sofa on the floor. He pressed the back of his hand against her forehead and decided she was a little on the warm side, so he only pulled a thin blanket over her before pressing a kiss to her cheek and going out to the front room to clean up the mess.

He marveled at the events of the evening. It had happened so quickly. He'd known that he would go through the portal somewhere in the vicinity of his mate, but he'd never imagined that his first interaction with her would be so stressful. He didn't think he'd ever been quite so worried for one person's well-being in his whole life.

After the wood floor was free of blood and he'd washed the blanket and towel and hung them to dry in the backyard, he went into the kitchen and opened his cooling unit. From inside the rectangular, metal-lined box, he pulled out packages of meat and set them on the marble counter, along with vegetables and fruit for juicing. He'd never cooked for anyone but himself before, but pride flared through him as he lit the thick ring of oil underneath the metal burner on his cooker and placed a pan on top to heat. After coating the pan with *wials* oil, he placed two thick blue-furred boar steaks in the pan and listened to them sizzle. He turned his attention to the fruit and sliced apart the green-fleshed *yumonmi*, twisting each half on the wooden juicer that drained into a small stone jug. When he'd juiced enough for several glasses, he set the jug in the cooling box to chill and flipped the steaks. He chopped vegetables, and after removing the steaks from the pan, he tossed the vegetables into the hot pan and cooked them until they were tender.

He plated the steaks and vegetables and set them on a tray inside the oven to keep warm. He put out the flame under the burner and washed his hands. He knew he needed to make a few calls, so while she was still asleep and since the sun was now up, he placed the calls. First, he opened a portal to call his father to share the news of his mate and the strange circumstances of their meeting.

"She's well now, though?" his father asked, his brow furrowing with concern.

"She's still unconscious, but yes, her leg is healed."

His father said, "Your mother will be back from the spa in six days. I would suggest that you head to the Mortal Realm before she returns. I will speak to her and let her know what's happened to you, and hopefully by the time you are ready to return here for your mating ceremony, she will realize how fortunate it is that you found your mate so quickly."

Crimson sighed. "Do you think she'll accept a she-wolf as my mate?"

His father's brow arched. "Does it matter?"

"Of course not. But I don't want Lindy to feel as if she doesn't belong with me just because mother wanted me to mate to a high-born female so she could go to all the high-society parties."

"The important thing is that you care for her and want her to be part of your life. Your mother will change her tune when you show her your first child. She melts around babes and will be helpless to deny her own grandchild."

Crimson couldn't help but smile at the thought of Lindy, pregnant with his child. Shifting his thoughts away from those that threatened to turn his cock to stone, he said goodbye to his father and promised to keep him updated on her condition. After ending the call with his father, he called his commanding officer and took a leave of absence to tend to his mate.

"I hadn't expected to come home so quickly, so I wanted to let you know that I'm still taking my leave of absence even though I'm home with my mate now."

"That's fine, Crimson. You're quite lucky to have found your mate so soon. I hope she recovers quickly from her injury."

Ending the call, he rolled his neck with a sigh and straightened up the kitchen before walking back to the bedroom. Lindy was still asleep. Although the part of him that had been raised a gentlemen didn't think he should crawl into bed with a nude, unconscious woman, the bigger, less-gentlemanly part of him decided that she was his mate and there was no better place for him to be than by her side. Even if she was naked.

The image of her pretty wolf form shifting back into her human form flashed through his mind. He'd caught a glimpse of her curvy body before he'd tossed a blanket over her to preserve her modesty in front of his friends. He couldn't wait to familiarize himself with every inch of her body.

He drew off his trousers and laid them over a leather armchair in the corner, extinguished the lights, and climbed gingerly into bed. Drawing the blanket up over his hip, he settled on his side and rested his hand on Lindy's stomach. The thin blanket separated his hand from her flesh, but he could feel the heat of her body against his palm, and it settled his beast to be able to touch her even in such a small way.

Closing his eyes, he fell asleep quickly, content that his mate was now home.

Chapter Nine

Lindy rolled over and shivered. She reached down for her comforter to pull it up over her shoulder but couldn't reach it. Yawning, she rolled to her back and stretched. As she lifted her arms up, one of her hands bumped into flesh, and she froze, her eyes popping open. She'd gone to bed alone last night, hadn't she? Wait. How had she even gotten into bed?

The wall in front of her looked like it was made of black stone. *That's not right.*

"You're safe now, Lindy," a male voice rumbled to her right.

She leapt off the bed as if it were on fire and slipped on a rug. As her legs went out from under her, strong arms prevented her from hitting the floor. He'd moved faster than her eyes could track. One minute he'd been in bed, and now he was setting her back on the bed.

"Calm down, Lindy. My name is Crimson, and I'm your truemate."

She looked at him in shock. "Excuse me?"

The corner of his mouth quirked up, and she forgot how to breathe. She'd never seen a more beautiful man in her life. He had short, dark brown hair, piercing green eyes, and a gorgeous body. Oh my. What a body.

"Did you really not hear me?" He raised one brow.

"I heard you. I just think you must be mistaken. I'm no one's truemate."

She shivered at his intense gaze and glanced down, quickly realizing she was naked as the day she was born.

Jerking a blanket around herself, she growled. "Just what the hell is going on here?"

"Crimson."

"What?"

"My name is Crimson."

She blew out a breath. "Fine. Crimson, what the hell is going on here?"

"Your truemate."

She clenched her teeth together. He was infuriating! She was naked and had no idea where she was or how she'd gotten here, and all he cared about was that she got his name right.

He smiled in a way that said he wouldn't tell her anything unless she cooperated.

"Look, Crimson, I'll say your name all you want, but I don't know you, and I don't know why you think I'm your truemate. We've never even met before. You can't possibly know."

He put his hands on his hips, and her gaze dropped without her permission to drink in his incredible body. Every inch of him was lean and muscular, and she couldn't stop herself from looking at his very erect cock. It took all of her willpower not to drop to her knees and see how good he would feel in her mouth.

Shit!

Shaking her head to clear the wicked images from her mind, she scooted back on the bed to put more distance between them.

"I know that you're mine, Lindy, because I spelled for you. I'm fae, and the spells aren't wrong."

He moved to come closer, and she put her hand up. "Put some pants on, please?"

He grinned. "Are you sure? It's more fun to talk when we're both naked."

"I'm sure. And where are my clothes?"

"Your clothes are wherever you left them before you went hunting on the full moon." He turned his back and walked through an archway. She ogled his ass while his back was turned and imagined how nice it would look with her fingernail marks on it. He came out of what must have been a closet with a pair of leather pants on. Instead of a zipper, the pants laced up the front and he'd conveniently forgotten to lace them closed.

"What do you remember about last night, *chelle?*"

Even though her hand was still up to keep him from getting too close, he sat down next to her anyway and kissed the top of her hand. Jerking it away from him, she willed her body to stop being so turned on by the stranger and thought back to the night before.

"I was hunting with Faith and Tina," she said, chewing on her bottom lip as her mind replayed the full moon. She remembered that Faith had barked a warning, and Lindy had seen the metal glinting in the moonlight but hadn't been able to stop in time. She jerked the blanket away to look at her leg, certain that it would be mangled beyond repair. But her right leg wasn't injured at all. She touched the smooth, unmarked skin in confusion.

"I don't understand."

He told her that he'd cast the spell for his truemate, and when he opened the portal, he'd felt compelled to shift into his beast form and he'd found her unconscious, bleeding, with a broken leg.

"I brought you here, and a healer in my glen helped to fix your leg. You shifted into your human form, and I brought you back to my bed. *Our* bed."

He wiggled his brows and smiled.

She ignored him. He was delusional. There was no way a hotter-than-hell guy like him was her truemate.

"Wait. You said you shifted into a beast? But you're a fairy, right?"

He nodded. "I'm a *wulfen*, which means I'm both fae and wolf. I am unique in this realm. And very lucky to find such a beautiful she-wolf to be my truemate."

"Why do you keep saying that I'm your truemate?" Hearing him say that word so many times was making her heart hurt.

"I already explained to you that I spelled for you. Besides the spell being infallible, I feel it in my bones that we're meant to be. My wolf wants to mark you and mate with you, and my fae side wants to follow the old ways and mate you in a grand ceremony."

She wasn't sure if she should blush at his bluntness or be turned on. Her body decided to keep going with *turned on*, and she cleared her throat and struggled to find something to say.

He chuckled. "I'm sorry if I'm being forward, but I don't believe in beating around the bush. When I decided to spell for you, I had planned to seduce you and convince you to come with me to my realm. But you're already here."

"So what, no seduction?" She slapped her hand over her mouth. Had she just said that?

He laughed, and she liked how it sounded when he was happy. He leaned forward slowly. His eyes shimmered, changing from green to red. "Oh, I'm going to seduce you, sweet Lindy, have no doubt about that. But not right now. I'm sure you're hungry."

He stood, and he was close enough that she could have reached out and touched his muscular abs. She clutched the blanket tighter to keep her hands to herself. She still didn't know what to think, and she was afraid to believe that something so amazingly wonderful had actually happened to her.

"I'll go get you the meal I prepared." He smiled once more and walked out of the room. She slumped back on the pillows and covered her eyes with her hands.

Taking in a deep breath, she let it out slowly and tried to decipher what had happened. She recalled hearing gossip in the pack about how Jenna had cast a spell for Logan and it had enabled him to be able to find her when they were mated. If what Crimson said was true, and he had spelled for her, then it was possible that he was her truemate, that his spell had led him right to her.

Her stomach flipped as elation warred with wariness inside her. Was it a horrible joke? Could it be true?

She closed her eyes and touched her wolf in her mind. Her beast growled in happiness, urging her to find the male that was in the house with them. When Lindy heard footsteps coming closer, her wolf began to pant and growl. Crimson walked into the room carrying a large plate in one hand, a stone pitcher in the other, and a cup tucked under his arm.

He paused at the foot of the bed. "Your eyes are amber, *chelle*. Are you all right?"

She forced the wolf down, worried that she was going to do something embarrassing like roll onto all fours and wiggle her ass. "I, um, my wolf was just scenting."

"She must like what she smells, huh?" He smiled broadly.

He put the plate down at the end of the bed and filled the glass with a green-tinted liquid. "It's sweet *yumonmi*. It reminds me of 7 Up," he said as he handed her the glass.

"You know what 7 Up is?"

"Sure. My uncle is mated to a human in a place called Orlando. I've visited them several times over the years. And when I graduated from the academy, a group of my friends and I spent a week in a place called Vegas and had a great time."

She took a long drink of the juice and found that he was right. Although not carbonated, it tasted like lemon-lime soda. He put the glass down on a side table and put the plate on his lap. Using a fork and knife, he cut a piece from a thick steak, speared a wedge of what looked like orange-colored zucchini, and held the fork up to her lips.

"I can feed myself," she said, reaching for the fork.

"I'm not done taking care of you, Lindy. You were seriously injured and unconscious for several hours. You're also my mate."

She considered arguing with him because she didn't want him to think that she was weak. But she'd never had a man feed her before. Or care that she was hurt. She opened her mouth, and he gently pushed the fork inside. The meat tasted wonderful, and the vegetable did taste like zucchini, even if it was oddly colored.

They didn't talk while he fed her both steaks and all the vegetables, but they didn't really need to talk. There was a connection between them that she was unable to deny. Her wolf wanted him, the darn thing wanted to roll to her back and let him scratch her tummy. Her human side was very attracted to him. More than the physical interest she had for him, she suddenly felt as if she couldn't handle being separated from him. He was definitely her truemate.

When she'd finished the last of the juice, she leaned back on the bed and put her hand on her stomach. "I'm stuffed. That was so good, thank you."

He put the plate on the floor. "It was my pleasure. Are you ready to talk yet?"

Her heart began to pound. "About what?"

"Us being truemates. Do you believe me?"

"I don't know you, but I do believe that we're mates."

"Truemates." He insisted.

She smiled. "Truemates."

"You'll get to know me as we spend time together, the same way that I'll get to know you, too. But, first, let me give you the grand tour, and then we'll go take a bath."

Bath?

He stood and went back into the closet and came out with a tunic. She slipped it over her head and found it quite a bit too big for her but made of very soft fabric. It also smelled like him, an intoxicating mixture of spice and musk.

He pulled her to her feet and made a sweeping gesture with his hand. "This is our bedroom. You remember the bed." He tilted his head and wiggled his brows with a grin. "This will become your favorite room in the house."

She didn't think she'd ever liked someone so quickly before, but she honestly just liked him. She laughed. "You're very sure of yourself."

He hummed. "There isn't anything I want more than to strip you bare and touch every inch of you with my fingers and tongue. I want you sated and boneless from pleasure." He pulled her close, and one hand closed around her waist while he linked the fingers of his other hand with hers. He kissed her ear and whispered, "Your scent drives me wild. I want to know what you sound like when you fall apart. I want to hear my name on your lips and feel your body clutching mine." As his lips smoothed down the column of her throat, her knees went weak, and her body throbbed. She thought she might come from the sound of his voice alone.

He groaned, and it shifted into a light growl. He placed a kiss on her throbbing pulse and straightened. His eyes were a mixture of green and red, like emeralds and rubies.

"Your eyes," she said, staring into the mesmerizing color.

"My beast has red eyes. When I'm feeling emotional, they'll change color. The same as yours."

She looked at their linked hands. His skin was tanner than hers, and she liked the contrast. "That never happened to me."

"Your eyes going to your wolf when you're human?"

"When I'm angry, yes, but not when I'm…"

His voice was laced with a growl when he tugged her even closer, and she felt the hard ridge of his arousal against her stomach. "Turned on?"

She couldn't find her voice, so she nodded.

"They're amber now, mixed with blue. Beautiful. Just like you."

Her body was going to combust. He was going to keep on saying the nicest, sexiest things she'd ever heard, and she was going to go up in flames and turn into a pile of ash on the floor.

He placed a soft kiss on her forehead, and she caught the hint of a smile on his lips. "Now for the rest of the tour."

He showed her the bathroom, which he called the *bathing room*. Like the bedroom, the walls were made of black stone. In one corner was a curtained area, and he pulled the curtain back to show her what looked like a primitive toilet. The base was carved out of the black stone and a wooden seat sat atop it. He showed her a lever in the wall next to the toilet, and when he pressed down on it, she could see the water rushing around the inside of the toilet base. He pushed up on the lever, and the water stopped. She'd never seen anything quite like it. The countertop was gray marble with the sink carved into it. Another lever allowed water to flow down into the sink.

"This is cleansing paste for your teeth. It's made from fairymint and is milder tasting than what you are used to." He touched the top of a small jar with a wooden toothbrush next to it. A mirror hung over the sink, and she saw the two of them together. He was taller than her five-feet-six by at least eight inches, lean and muscular where she was curved and soft. Her mind began to compare them, casting doubts on the truemating that he seemed so certain of. Her wolf snarled the worries away. Each minute that passed made her more aware of a connection between them that was unlike anything she had ever experienced before.

He pointed out the tub. It was huge and oval shaped and appeared to be carved out of the wall. The black stone was polished so it shone like glass. It was at least big enough for two people. His fingertips skimmed down the backs of her arms as he whispered in her ear, "That's not where we're going to bathe today, Lindy."

She shivered from head to toe. "No?"

"Another time yes, but not today."

He pulled towels from a shelf along one wall and grabbed a bar of soap from the counter that was white streaked with pink, tucking the bundle under one arm. He took her hand and tugged her out of the bathroom, through the bedroom, and into a hallway. Another, smaller, bedroom was across the hall and was empty except for a rocking chair made of bent tree branches.

The main room had a sofa made out of an animal hide that she was betting was from an animal she'd never heard of before. A low table, made of a polished section of tree trunk, sat in front of the sofa. She noticed there were no lamps or overhead lights, only candles, lanterns, and sconces. When he showed her the kitchen, which contained another sink with a lever for the water source, a cook-top stove with some sort of oil underneath the burners, and a fridge carved of stone, she knew she'd never been inside a home like this before.

"You don't have electricity?"

He leaned against the small square table. "No. We don't have vehicles, either." At her confused look, he smiled and said, "We use horses and carriages. I've heard that women from the Mortal Realm tend to think of it as quaint."

At the mention of other women, her wolf growled in jealousy. Crimson's eyes widened, and he shook his head, pulling her into his arms and placing a kiss on her forehead. "I didn't mean that I've brought any women from the Mortal Realm here, sweetling, but there are women from your realm here that are mated to fae." His hands stroked up and down her back, and the tension eased from her. His voice lowered into a whisper, "Do you think I'd be so crass as to mention something of that nature so casually? There will be time to talk about our pasts, but not now."

She nodded as a knot of fear lodged in her stomach. What would he think about her past? The way that she had tried so hard to fuck her way into a mating with a highly ranked male? And, worse, the way that no male of worth in her pack had wanted anything to do with her? Shame filled her. She wished she could go back in time and save herself for Crimson, so she could be just his.

He tipped her chin up, frowning. She felt like he could read her mind, and she was ashamed of all that she'd done. He brushed his thumb across her lower lip, tracing the edge. "Your past doesn't matter to me, Lindy. Our life together began the moment I picked you up in my arms. Whatever you did before only matters in the sense that it shaped you into the beautiful woman in my arms and brought us together. Whatever is troubling you, let it go. Nothing—*nothing*—will ever change the fact that we are truemates and meant to be together. Do you understand?"

Relieved tears stung her eyes, and she blinked quickly and nodded. He kissed her, just once, a simple press of his lips to hers. Picking up the bundle he had set on the table, he took her hand and led her to the front door. He stepped into a pair of leather shoes that reminded her of moccasins and told her to do the same with a slightly smaller pair that he said he had purchased earlier in the week when he knew he was going to find his truemate.

"It's not far to the hot springs, I thought we could walk," he said, opening the door and ushering her out. The sun was setting, turning the sky a pretty gold color.

"How long was I unconscious for?"

"Past lunch, why?"

"It just seems early for the sun to be setting," she mused.

"I suppose it is for your realm, but things are different here in the Fae Realm. You'll get used to it."

She paused, and he stopped to look down at her. "What's wrong?"

"I've been gone almost a day?"

"Not quite. Why?"

"Do my friends even know that you took me?" She knew that Faith would never have left her if she were injured. She would have stayed right by her side no matter what.

He looked uncomfortable. "I told the woman who was with you that I was going to take care of you. You were bleeding to death so I just broke the trap and took you through the portal back to my realm."

Alarm filled her. "I have to let them know I'm okay!" She turned to run back into the house, but he grabbed her arm.

"It's not as if you can use one of those cell phones to call them, Lindy. We're in a different *realm*."

The way he said realm made her feel like she'd been taken to another planet. "You brought me here. Take me back."

His eyes narrowed, and his body tensed. "I will not." His eyes began to change color, and his lips pulled back in a possessive snarl. "You're mine."

She frowned and tried to step away from him, but his grip on her arm prevented her from moving. "I didn't say I wasn't yours, Crimson, but my friend Faith was with me, and she's probably worried sick."

He relaxed fractionally, but his eyes stayed red mixed with green. "It's too late. In the morning, I'll take you back so you can reassure your friends that you're safe, and then we'll come back."

Suspicion roared inside her. She stepped away and pulled her arm free of his hand. "Why are you acting as if I'm going to live here forever?"

He frowned. "We're truemates. Where else would you live?"

"In my house in my realm."

The elation she'd felt since she'd realized that Crimson was her mate was evaporating quickly. He closed the distance between them with one step, his body brushing against hers. "Don't be upset, Lindy. I hadn't really thought any further than you being here with me."

Well, things *had* moved pretty quickly over the last day. "I have a job, friends, my pack, my mom…all of that is back in the Mortal Realm. Right now I don't know you well enough to say that I want to be here permanently."

He seemed to will himself to calm down as she watched the red slowly fade from his green eyes. "I'll take you back tomorrow morning for a few hours so you can speak to whoever you need to. But promise to come back here with me for a few days, and then we can spend time in your realm. Maybe you'll want to live here instead, or maybe I'll want to live there." He placed one hand on her neck and stroked his thumb along her jaw. "We have the rest of our lives, Lindy. We don't have to make any decisions today."

She stared into his eyes and felt the truth of his words. He was an interesting mixture of possessive wolf and honorable gentleman.

"I promise we can come back here for a while. I'm sorry I jumped to conclusions," she said.

"I'm sorry I gave you a reason to do so." He picked up her hand and kissed it. "Let's go relax."

They walked away from the house on a stone path that led to a paved road. Crossing the road, they stepped onto another stone path and followed it across a narrow strip of thick grass until they passed into woods. The trees were thick and tall, with white-and-gray-striped bark. Her hand tightened in his as they moved deeper into the woods, and her wolf was on alert, but she felt safe with Crimson and knew that he would protect her.

Because they were truemates.

Chapter Ten

Crimson didn't expect to find anyone at the hot springs. Most of the warriors used the springs after training to soothe overused muscles, and training for the day had ended several hours earlier. Some of his fellow warriors were mated, however, and it wasn't uncommon for males to bring their females to the springs to bathe from time to time.

The springs came into view, and Lindy's appreciative gasp was music to his ears. Steam rose from the surface of the water. Smooth, multi-colored stones edged the pool, and thick grass surrounded it. The bottom of the pool was made of fine, black sand.

He put the towels and bar of honeysuckle soap down on one of the stones and stepped from his shoes. Tugging his shirt over his head, he folded it and set it on the grass then turned her to face him. His beast practically pranced as her eyes dropped immediately to his bare chest and darkened with pleasure.

"The springs have been here for millennia. The water has healing properties. When I first trained with the military, some of the old soldiers said that water nymphs used to come here at night and dance naked on the surface."

She glanced at the water and then back to him with a smile. "Was that so the young recruits would spend the night hiding, hoping to see naked nymphs?"

He chuckled. "How did you know?"

She smiled. "When I first shifted, my grandfather and some of his friends took me and some of my cousins out to teach us to hunt. He said we were going to hunt 'snipe', which he assured us was a tasty, easy-to-catch bird. The three of us stood there in our wolf forms, waiting for the adults to chase the birds out of the shrubs, but instead they came racing out banging wooden spoons on metal pots, yelling that the snipe were getting away. My cousins and I raced around trying to find these elusive birds, but no matter how many times the adults told us where they were, we never saw them. Eventually we heard the adults laughing and realized that the 'snipe hunt' was just for fun. Apparently snipe aren't real."

He liked hearing about her past even though he could tell that she was ashamed of something. He didn't think she was a virgin, so he assumed she'd had many partners and thought he would be put off by that. He wasn't, because he was no innocent either. As long as she understood they were each other's only from now on, her past—and his as well—was going to remain exactly that. In the past.

He reached for the hem of her top, and she made a startled sound and stepped back. "What are you doing?"

He jerked his head toward the water. "Taking care of you."

She bit her lower lip with her top teeth. His wolf growled at the sight. "I, uh, you're going to see me naked?"

Aw, his mate was shy.

"I've already seen you naked," he pointed out. "When you shifted, I saw your beautiful, creamy white skin and the soft curves that make my hands ache with the need to touch." He played his fingers along her neck, and she shivered. "I can see you naked anytime I want."

Her eyes narrowed. "Excuse me?"

"Sure. In my head, see?" He closed his eyes. "Oh yeah, there you are. Naked. Naked and all mine."

She slapped him playfully on the arm and laughed. "Crimson!"

He opened his eyes and captured her face between his hands. Lowering his mouth, he brushed his lips against hers and felt like crowing to the sky when her lips parted on a sigh and she leaned against him. He slipped his tongue into her mouth and touched hers, deepening the kiss. He dropped one hand from her face to her waist, pulling her closer as their tongues slid together in an erotic dance. The scent of her arousal pulsed in the air around them, and he wanted to strip her bare and make love to her right there on the bank of the hot springs.

Leashing his wolf, he pulled away from the drugging kiss. Her eyes were closed and her lips were swollen and parted, her cheeks pink with a blush. He didn't want to make love to her for the first time outside where someone might see them. He was going to treat her right and continue to take care of her, no matter how badly his wolf panted.

He hadn't laced his trousers earlier, so he simply pushed them down his legs and stepped out of them, tossing them toward his shirt and shoes. From the tension in her body, he could tell she was trying not to look at his cock. Part of him wanted her to look and touch and do whatever else her mind could dream up. But not here. This time she didn't protest when he pinched the hem of the shirt in his fingers and lifted it up her body. He swore the woods around them went quiet as he tugged the shirt over her head and dropped it to the grass, and unlike her, he had no qualms about staring at his mate's perfect body.

His eyesight was quite sharp thanks to his wolf, and he could see her as clearly as if it were daytime. The full heaviness of her breasts. The sleek curve of her waist. His gaze drank her in like a man dying of thirst. He'd truly never seen a more beautiful woman in his life. Everything about her spoke to him on a cellular level.

"How did I get so lucky?" He kissed her once, knelt to grab the bar of soap and a small cloth, and then straightened, taking her hand.

She didn't answer, but a glance at her told him she was pleased he liked the way she looked. He pulled her with him a few feet to where a set of steps had been carved into the rocks, and he stepped down into the water.

"Oh," she said in surprise as she moved down to the first step. "It's perfect."

He agreed, and not just about the water. She mirrored him as he slowly moved down into the water and out into the pool. At the deepest end it was almost ten feet deep and under a foot deep at the shallowest end. He stopped when the water was above his waist. He cast his hearing out to make sure they were still alone, and when his wolf was satisfied that no one else was around, he ducked under the water and urged her to do the same.

As she surfaced, smoothing her hair back with her hands, the moonlight caught the water on her body, and she looked exactly as he'd pictured the water nymphs looking like all those years ago. His wolf rose up inside him quickly, and the need to mark her and make her his forever was almost too hard to ignore. He fought the urge to turn her around and sink his teeth into her neck and bury his cock deep inside her pussy. With some effort, he turned his attention to the soap and lathered his hands. He buried his fingers into her wet tresses and began to work the soap into a thick lather. Her head tipped back, and she gripped his upper arms as her eyes slid closed with a soft groan. He'd never witnessed anything so erotic in his life. He washed her hair and then, as she rinsed it out under the water, he reached for the cloth underwater and then grabbed the soap that had been floating on the water next to them.

She smoothed her hair back and smiled at him. "What kind of soap is that? It smells really nice."

"Honeysuckle. I'm glad you like it."

He dropped the soap and picked up her hand. He washed each of her fingers and then her hand before stroking the cloth up her arm slowly. Swirling the cloth across her chest, he tended to her other arm before smoothing the lather onto her stomach. He reached for the soap and lathered the cloth again, making sure that his hands were well lathered, too. He pressed the cloth and one lathered hand against her waist and slid his hands slowly up her body. Her eyes never left his, but her hands dug into his upper arms, and her mouth parted slightly as he moved his hands to her breasts. The cloth covered one mound, but his other hand captured the swell. Her nipple pebbled against his thumb as he rubbed the lather onto her skin. The cloth slipped into the water, and he cupped both of her breasts with his hands, all pretense of cleaning gone.

Her breasts were large but fit perfectly in his hands as he stroked his thumbs across her tight nipples. He hadn't meant to turn the simple act of bathing his mate into part of the seduction he'd planned for her, but the sight of her in the moonlight, glistening with water and staring up at him with eyes so full of awe made him want to lay her down on the grass and make love to her now.

Her hands slid up his arms to his shoulders, and he lowered his head to press his lips against hers. One of his hands slid around her back to pull her close as he slipped his tongue into her mouth and slid it against hers. She moaned, and the sound rushed to his cock. He gently pinched her nipple between his finger and thumb, tugging on the peak. Her body writhed against his.

Inching his hand down her soap-slicked stomach, he pushed his hand below the water. She parted her legs and sucked on his tongue, and he didn't have to be a psychic to know that she wanted him to touch her, maybe as much as he wanted to touch her.

He slid his finger between the soft lips of her sex. He traced the edges of her folds and circled her clit. Her hips moved, pressing against his hand, and he smiled as her hands slid up to his neck and her nails dug into his flesh. Just as his finger circled the hot entrance to her body, his wolf growled, and he jerked her behind him, facing into the darkened woods.

Riyad, Merik, and two females walked from the woods, and he straightened from the defensive stance, but kept his arm around Lindy, holding her to his back. He didn't want anyone to see her naked except him.

"Sorry, Crim," Riyad said. "I didn't think we'd see you out of your house so soon."

Crimson didn't expect Riyad, or anyone else, to understand what his wolf was compelled to do to take care of his mate, and he wasn't going to explain things to them. At least not now.

The sensual tone of the bath had taken a nose-dive since his friends had intruded, and now he only wanted to take her home. "Give us a minute of privacy, please?"

Merik made an annoyed sound, but Riyad shoved his shoulder, and the small group turned away from him and Lindy. He turned and scooped water into his hands and poured it over her shoulders to rid her body of the soap. As he gathered the cloth and soap that were floating nearby, he grabbed her hand and tugged her up the steps, keeping her body shielded with his own. His wolf was snapping to make the males leave the area, but he kept his mouth shut and wrapped one of the thick towels around her. He shoved his feet into his shoes and tucked a towel around his waist, gathering their clothes into a bundle with the wet cloth and soap, and then said over his shoulder, "Thanks," as he hurried her into the woods.

It hadn't escaped his notice, as he was rushing to get her away from the two single males, that the sexy look had faded quickly from her eyes, replaced with unhappiness.

He stopped on the stone patio behind his home and willed a lantern over the door to light. She looked up at it in surprise.

"Did you do that?"

"Yes, what's wrong?"

"How did you do that?" She wasn't looking at him, but at the flickering flame.

He dropped their things and cupped her face, turning her to look at him. "My fae power is controlling flames. Now, what's wrong?"

Her brows rose. "Nothing. I just didn't know how the light came on."

He huffed. "Not that. What was wrong before?"

Her brows furrowed, and then she pressed her lips together, darting her eyes to the side. "Nothing."

Growling, he waited until she looked at him again. "I can see that you're upset, and it's making my wolf go nuts. Is it because of the males? I did my best to keep them from seeing you." If she was upset, he clearly hadn't done a good job of protecting her.

Her voice was bitter when she said, "I doubt they saw me, which was what you wanted, right?"

"Of course I didn't want them to see you. You're mine. I don't want any other males to see your unclothed body. It was all I could do to get you away from there without throttling my friends."

Her mouth fell open in surprise. "You aren't ashamed to be seen with me?"

He'd never been more confused in his life. "What in hades are you talking about, *chelle*?"

A relieved smile lit her face, and then her cheeks darkened in a blush. "I thought you might be ashamed of me."

He felt his fangs elongate in anger. His rush to get her away from prying eyes had led her to believe that he was embarrassed to be seen with her. Who had filled her head with such nonsense and made her believe she should expect to be treated so poorly?

He opened the door and ushered her inside, trying to calm down the wolf that wanted to race into her realm and hurt whoever had made her feel so badly about herself. Slamming the door, he dropped their things and lifted her into his arms, pushing her back against the door. Her legs immediately went around his waist, and her hands clutched at his shoulders. He ground his erection into the apex of her thighs, the towels between them doing nothing to spare her the feeling of his hard cock. "I was so distracted by you, so intent on making you come, that I almost let two unmated males see your naked body. It's not that I'm ashamed of you in any way, because I'm not. But I absolutely will not allow anyone – wolf, fae, human, or other – to see your beautiful, bare body."

Her head fell back against the door with a soft thud, and she tightened her legs around his waist. "I'm sorry."

"It was my fault. I knew I'd be too tempted to keep from touching you intimately. I apologize for making you feel bad. I'm proud to have you as my mate, but your body is for me alone."

A tiny smile curved her full lips, and her eyes darkened with passion. "Just so you know, the possessiveness goes both ways."

He was glad that she didn't want anyone to see him, too.

Pulling away from the door, he carried her into the bedroom and put her down on the bed. After bringing her a clean top, he pulled on his trousers, put their things away, and joined her on the bed. Although he desperately wanted to go back to touching and kissing her, he didn't want her to believe that all he wanted from her was sex. He wanted to know everything about her and share all about himself. He couldn't recall ever feeling like this before, and he knew it was the powerful connection of truemates. There would never be another female for him, and he would slaughter anyone who touched her.

She had grown up in a pack in Allen, Kentucky, which, according to her was in the Midwest. He knew enough from traveling to the Mortal Realm where the Midwest was, although he had never been to Kentucky, except for when he had come to her rescue. Her mother had left the pack several years ago and had urged Lindy to join her, but she hadn't wanted to leave her job or her friends.

She hesitated in her story, and he squeezed her hand. "I want to know everything, Lindy. I don't want to go into our mating with secrets. Nothing you say will change how I feel about you, but I will be angry if you keep things from me."

Taking a deep breath, she began to tell him about the vast emptiness that she had started to feel. She'd gotten a reputation in the pack for being promiscuous, what the males referred to as a "toy", but slowly the attention had become empty, making her feel lonelier. No males saw her as anything but a few hours in bed, and aside from her two best friends, most females considered her trash. When she'd grown tired of the meaningless sex, she'd tried to find a male to mate with her. Even though she knew that none of the single males in her pack were her truemate, she'd felt desperately lonely, afraid that she'd wind up alone for the rest of her life.

She sat next to him on the bed with her hands twisted in the blanket and wouldn't meet his eyes. He could see that she was worried about what he would think of her when she finished the story of her life.

"I just don't get it," he said.

She met his eyes. "Get what?"

"How any male could be with you once and not want to stay forever." He leaned closer. "You're sweet. Kind. Beautiful. That the males couldn't see below the surface to the enticing, loving female I know you are is their loss."

Her eyes widened in surprise, and she threw herself into his arms and hugged him tightly around the neck. Hugging her back, he said, "It's true, Lindy. I wouldn't want anyone else but you, and I've known you for less than a day. You're mine forever."

She laughed, but he could tell she was struggling not to cry. His mate had a tender heart, and she'd been treated poorly for too long. All of that changed the moment he spelled for her. He'd treat her with respect, and some day he'd earn her trust and her love.

"Thank you," she whispered with a thick voice.

"For what?" He rubbed his hands up and down her back.

She leaned away slightly, and he reached up and brushed the tears from her cheeks. "For being understanding."

"It's my pleasure." He brushed his lips across hers. Casting a glance at the wall clock, he saw it was well past midnight.

"If you want to go back to your pack in the morning, we should get some rest." He pulled back the covers and settled next to her. She was still sitting up and looked down at him. "What about your life story?"

He held out his arms and beckoned her to lie down with him, which she did. She stretched out next to him, laying her head on his shoulder and resting one arm across his stomach. "I'll tell you everything tomorrow. If I start my story now, we'll never get any sleep."

She yawned and snuggled closer, and he willed the lights off. The room slipped into darkness, and he closed his eyes, grateful to be holding his mate in his arms.

Chapter Eleven

They stood outside Crimson's home, and he looked like an angel dropped from heaven. Brilliant white-feathered wings rose from his back like silken shields, and his bare upper body was lean and muscular. Scars dotted his skin in places along his arms and chest, and when she had asked about them, he said they were from when he trained as a youth.

"Go ahead, you can touch them," he said, placing his hands on his hips.

She walked around and stood at his back. The tops of the wings reached above his ears and stretched out several feet on either side of his body.

"Can you fly?" She placed her hands on the area where the wings jutted from his shoulders.

"Yes. Only warrior fae have feathered wings and can fly. Civilian fae have wings that are made of thin membranes and can be quite colorful."

Stroking her hands up, she felt the bumpy texture of the skin covering the bones, and then she ran the backs of her hands down the feathers, marveling at their soft texture.

"They're beautiful, Crimson," she said.

"When we come home, I'll take you for a ride if you'd like." She moved around to face him, smiling at his enthusiasm. "You're not afraid of heights, are you?"

"As long as you don't drop me, no."

He sobered quickly. "I would never."

Rolling her eyes, she said, "I was just teasing. I trust you. It's strange because I've never really trusted anyone as quickly as I do you. But I know, deep down, that you're a male of honor and that I can trust you."

"It's our truemate connection. When we mate, the connection will grow even stronger."

The night before, when she'd laid out her life for him, ashamed to hear herself say all of the things she'd done in her misguided efforts to find a mate, she'd expected he would be unhappy with her behavior. But he had been surprisingly understanding. And then he wanted to just sleep instead of having sex. Before meeting him, the *old* her would have believed that she'd done or said something to turn him off. But now she knew that he was simply taking his time and not rushing forward into the mating. She'd never had a male be so considerate. In her wildest fantasies, she'd never thought she would find such a perfect mate.

She went up on her toes, and he bent his head and kissed her. Hand in hand, they walked back through the grass to an area that he said was his "fairy ring," formed with rocks. Only he could use it, he explained, because it was his private ring. No one from the Mortal Realm could come through it without him, and no one from the Fae Realm could use it either.

He settled on his knees, and she stood next to him, watching in fascination as he placed his hands in the air and closed his eyes. The air in front of him began to shimmer and grow slowly opaque, and then it cleared, and she was staring into the woods in her pack's territory. The portal lengthened and widened until it was the size of a door, and he lowered his hands and stood.

"Does that make you tired?" she asked, taking his offered hand.

"No. When my wings are out, my fae powers are stronger. It would take a great deal of effort to exhaust me." He smiled down at her. "Don't be nervous. It won't hurt to go through the portal."

"I trust you," she said.

He grinned and squeezed her hand. He stepped through the portal and pulled her with him. It felt like she was stepping into cold, thick air as she left the Fae Realm and entered the woods in her pack's territory.

They walked to the full moon meeting place where she'd left her clothes before she shifted with her packmates. She kept on Crimson's tunic but pulled on her panties and shorts, slipping her feet into her flip-flops and carrying her top and the shoes he let her use. Taking his hand, she said, "We should check in with my alphas, and then go back to my home."

He didn't say anything as they walked the hundred yards to Jason and Cades' home. When the house came into view, she saw Jason sitting on the deck with his daughter, Lyric, in his lap and his cell in one hand. His eyes widened, and he put the phone in his pocket before standing and gathering his daughter close. He called for Cades and said, "Lindy! The pack's been worried sick! Are you all right?"

Cadence came out of the house. "Lindy!" She walked quickly to them, gathering Lindy in a hug. "Are you okay?"

Lindy was overwhelmed by their concern. "It's a bit of a long story."

Cades nodded, looking at Crimson. "Then come inside. I was just getting breakfast on the table."

Once inside, Lindy introduced Crimson to her alphas. Jason put Lyric in her booster seat as Cades motioned her and Crimson to the table to sit down. Within minutes, she and Jason joined them.

Jason put his elbows on the table and folded his hands. "What happened?"

Lindy had always known that Jason was a good alpha, but seeing him concerned for her welfare made her see him in a whole new light. He could have just sent her on her way, but instead, he and his mate opened up their home and were genuinely interested in what had happened.

She told them what she remembered of getting caught in the trap, and then Crimson filled in the rest. When the meal was over, Jason leaned back in his chair and said, "It's a good thing you spelled for Lindy when you did."

Crimson took her hand under the table and rested it on his thigh. "I'm grateful for that."

Jason said, "One of our wolves is mated to a she-fairy. They're actually in the Fae Realm looking for you, Lindy."

Her surprise must have shown on her face because Cades smiled softly. "You're part of the pack, Lindy, and you were injured and then taken. Of course we care."

Emotion welled up in Lindy, and she almost started to cry, but she managed to stave off the tears. "Thank you. I need to get home and call Faith and McKenna."

"I'll send Teller over to Logan's home," Jason said, reaching into his pocket for his phone.

At her confused look, Jason said, "There's a sprite that lives in Jenna's garden, and she can find Jenna in the Fae Realm and tell her that you're home."

Cades walked her and Crimson out the front door to where Lindy's car was parked. "Are you staying in the pack, or are you going to live in the Fae Realm?" Cades asked.

Lindy pulled her car keys from her pocket. "I don't know what's going to happen."

Crimson said, "If it's all right with you, Cadence, Lindy is going to come back with me to my realm for a week, and then we'll come back here for a while. That way we can both make an informed decision on where we'll be living permanently."

Cades smiled in relief. "Oh, okay, that sounds fine. Let me know if you need anything."

Lindy promised that she would keep her alphas in the loop and sat down behind the wheel. Crimson shut her door and then walked around the front, opening the passenger door and sitting down.

As she drove away from her alpha's home, she said, "A week?"

"You have to make an informed decision, *chelle*."

She glanced at him. He was watching out the window. "What if I want to live here?"

He met her eyes with a smile. "Then we will." He reached for her hand again and kissed the top. "I'm just asking you to be open-minded."

She was sure that she could live in a cardboard box in an alley and she'd be happy to be with him. In some ways, that thought was frightening to her because she'd never cared about someone so quickly. But knowing that he was her truemate eased her fears. Even if she didn't really know him yet, her soul knew him and her wolf trusted him, and that was enough to chase the cloudy thoughts away.

When she reached her small home, she immediately called Faith, who promised to get McKenna and come straight over to see for themselves that she was okay and hear what had happened. She couldn't have prevented them from coming over with a ten-foot-high electric fence around her place, so she gave Crimson a tour of her home and opened up the fridge to make lunch.

"I'll cook for you, *chelle*," he offered, looking over her shoulder at the contents on the shelves.

"You took good care of me when I was at your home. Let me do the same for you, here."

He seemed to consider it for a moment and then said, "When we've decided where we'll live permanently, promise me that we'll share the household responsibilities and that you'll let me spoil you whenever I feel like it."

She grinned and began pulling items from the refrigerator. "I promise."

He kissed her neck. "I might feel like it all the time."

Chuckling, she turned from the fridge and closed the door. "I promise to let you all the time."

"Good." He grinned, and her pulse sped up. He had the sexiest smile.

By the time she had sliced chicken breasts and sautéed them in a pan, McKenna, Drake, and Faith had arrived. After hugging her, both women demanded to know what had happened.

Faith looked at Crimson accusingly. "You! You're the one who stole my best friend!"

Lindy stepped in front of Crimson and put her hands up. "He saved my life, Faith. You know he did. You saw the trap and how injured I was. If Crimson hadn't shown up when he did, I could have died or been lame the rest of my life."

"I'm sorry that I couldn't stop to tell you what I was doing, but I knew I had to get Lindy to safety as quickly as possible," Crimson said, wrapping his arms around Lindy and resting his chin on top of her head. She rubbed her palms along his arms.

McKenna said, "So you guys are mated now? When did that happen?"

Lindy said, "Not officially yet, but yes, we're mates." Wolves didn't consider themselves fully, officially mated until they had sex and marked each other with their fangs. Just the thought of sinking her fangs into Crimson's neck made her teeth tingle in anticipation.

McKenna nodded and then tossed her long, black hair over her shoulder. "Are you making fajitas? I'm starving."

Faith's mouth, previously in a scowl, pulled up at the corners. "Fajitas? Me, too!"

While Lindy cut and roasted vegetables, Faith set the table for five, and McKenna grilled Crimson on the Fae Realm and his plans. Drake watched from his seat at the table with an amused expression. Lindy listened with a smile as McKenna proved what a good, protective friend she was and Crimson answered each question honestly and sincerely.

As Lindy put down the platter of chicken and vegetables, Crimson said, "I swear on my life that I will go to my grave to see Lindy safe and happy. You have nothing to fear from me when it comes to her, except that my overprotective wolf won't tolerate her being in danger."

Lindy sat down next to him at her small table, and her friends sat across from them. McKenna and Faith seemed to have changed their tune when it came to Crimson. He had really won them over. And it probably helped that he was sexy as hell and as sweet as candy.

After she showed Crimson how to make a fajita, they spent the meal discussing the trap she'd been caught by and what was happening with the pack. None of the local farmers who owned land butting up to the pack's territory would claim the traps. So far, two traps had been found. The first one had been just at the edge of the territory, but the one that had caught her was fairly deep into their territory. One trap was possibly an accident. Maybe the person who placed it didn't realize how close to pack territory it was. But two of the same kind of trap showing up within weeks of each other was deliberate.

While Faith and McKenna did the dishes, Lindy boxed up the leftovers for Faith and Mac to take home with them. "Do you have to leave?" Faith asked over her shoulder.

"I'm spending a week in the Fae Realm to see what it's like, and then we'll be back here."

McKenna dried a plate and put it away. Then she turned her back to the counter and crossed her arms over her chest. "You might move there, though."

Lindy shrugged. Hours earlier she'd been incensed that Crimson wanted her to live with him in the other realm permanently. But the more time she spent with him, the more she realized she didn't really care where they lived as long as they were together. If he wanted to live in the other realm, she knew she wouldn't fight it. She would be sad to leave this life behind, especially since she had just begun to enjoy herself with the pack again, but Crimson was her mate. Wherever he was—no matter the realm—was going to be home for her.

They finished the dishes in silence, and then Faith hugged Lindy as they stood at the front door. "When you come back, we're going to make sure Crimson has such a good time here with the pack that he won't want to live anywhere else."

McKenna echoed the statement. "You're my sister in the pack and my best friend. I don't know what I'd do without you."

Lindy felt her eyes sting at their declarations as she waved goodbye and shut the door, leaning her head against the cool wood. Crimson's hands settled on her shoulders, and he massaged them lightly. "You have wonderful friends, *chelle*."

"What does that word mean?" She turned in his arms and rubbed her cheek against his chest.

"Sweetheart."

The silence settled around them. She felt as if there were a thousand things she needed to say to him, but her mouth wouldn't open. If she'd been able to speak, she might have told him she didn't want to live in his realm and be away from her best friends and her pack, but she might also have been as likely to tell him she would be happy to live in his realm because she could make a home with him anywhere. But she didn't say anything as she stood in his arms, drinking in the darkly sweet scent of him and feeling the strength of his arms. She didn't have to make a decision now. They had a week to spend in his realm. Maybe she'd love it. Maybe she'd hate it. Whatever came at the end of the week, nothing was set in stone, and as long as they were together, they could figure out all the complicated stuff later.

"Want help packing a bag?" he asked after several quiet minutes.

"Sure."

She led him back to the bedroom, and he retrieved a medium-sized rolling suitcase from the top shelf of the closet. He put it on the bed and unzipped it. After a discussion on the similarities of the two realms' weather patterns, she packed tops and shorts and two sundresses.

"Just how many shoes do you need, *chelle*?" he asked with an amused smile as she tucked tennis shoes and two pairs of sandals into the bag.

"I like to be prepared," she said as she walked into the bathroom and grabbed her toiletry bag from under the cabinet and began to fill it with makeup.

"It's just a week," he said.

Men.

She came out of the bathroom zipping up the small bag and tossed it into the open suitcase. "What do female fairies wear?"

He zipped up the case. "Dresses or long tops and skirts. I think you might call it old-fashioned."

She'd been wearing miniskirts and skin-baring tops since she was sixteen. She liked the idea of old-fashioned clothing.

He went into the backyard, and she followed him a few minutes later after contacting her boss, Stella, to let her know she'd be taking a week off work and making sure the house was locked. She found him arranging rocks from the flowerbed into a crude circle in front of a three-foot dogwood tree.

His shirt was off, and his wings were out. He brushed his hand free of dirt and said, "Come on, *chelle*, we need to get going."

She joined him and watched as he opened the portal with his power. Through the portal she could see his house. "In a hurry?"

"To get you home so we can pick up where we left off last night in the hot springs."

Her cheeks heated with a blush as she remembered the very sexy bath he'd been giving her. Laughing, he stood, took her hand, and pulled her through the portal.

He carried her over the threshold of the house then retrieved the suitcase from where it had dropped to the ground. In the bedroom, he willed a light on in the closet and said, "Make yourself at home. I'll get us something to drink."

The closet was spectacular. It was carved from the same dark stone as the rest of the house. Drawers and shelves were built into one long wall with tops and pants hanging from wooden bars. She opened her bag and hung up her dresses and tops then folded her shorts neatly on one of the empty shelves. Her clothes looked strange next to his. Black leather trousers hung next to rustic tunics and vests. Her floral sundresses seemed completely out of place, as if they were from another time. After putting her undergarments in an empty drawer and her shoes on a low shelf, she unpacked her toiletries into a drawer in the bathroom and put her empty suitcase against the wall in the closet, out of the way.

Crimson came back into the bedroom with two glasses of peach-tinted liquid and handed one to her.

"To the next week." He tapped the rim of his glass against hers.

She took a sip and made a pleased sound. It tasted like apricots. "This is good. What's it called?"

"*Frioa* juice. It's my favorite."

"It might become mine, too."

She watched him over the lip of her glass as she took another drink. He was so sexy. Her wolf rumbled in agreement. Her teeth tingled again, the urge to sink her fangs into his neck rising fast and hard. He took the glass from her and set it on the small table next to the bed then, before she could blink, she was in his arms and his mouth was on hers. Her hands gripped his shoulders as he angled his head and deepened their kiss. His tongue danced against hers, sliding into her mouth like he was fucking her and not kissing her. Her hips tilted in invitation, and he ground his erection against her.

Leaving her mouth, he kissed down her neck with a light growl, his teeth nipping her flesh and making her nerve-endings go haywire. She grabbed the bottom of his shirt, pulled it free from the confines of his pants, and shoved it upward, anxious to feel his skin under her fingers. He lifted from her neck for only long enough to pull the shirt over his head then he growled again, his eyes flashing from green to red.

"You, too." His voice was gravelly.

She couldn't take her eyes off him as she lifted the tunic over her head and dropped it to the floor. His hands curled into fists, and his knuckles turned white. "Get in bed, *chelle*," he demanded with a harsh whisper. His voice cascaded over her, rippling down her spine like a caress.

She turned to the bed and jerked the covers back. Something hissed. She looked down at the mattress and screamed as a black-scaled snake lunged at her, jaws wide and fangs gleaming.

Crimson pushed her out of the way as a sword appeared in his hand. He swung the sword down, and the snake's head dropped to the floor with a wet thud, the jaws still working. The body writhed on the bed as olive-colored blood spurted from the wound, and Lindy covered her nose with her hand as an acrid scent filled the room.

Crimson used his free hand to pull the covers away completely, but the snake appeared to be alone. He took in a deep breath and cracked his neck, and when he looked at her, she could see that his eyes were completely red. "Are you all right?"

"Scared out of my mind, but yeah. What is that thing?"

"A maw-serpent." He speared the head with his sword and dropped it next to the body before the sword disappeared from his hand. The creature was several feet long, and the head was the size of her fist. He gathered the creature in the covers and went into the bathroom. She heard him say something under his breath, and then she smelled something burning. She peeked into the bathroom and saw that he'd put the covers in the tub, setting them on fire with his fae power.

He lifted his hands, and the flames turned from orange to blue, the radiant heat so great that she had to retreat into the bedroom. Warily, she looked at the bed. She could have climbed under the covers without pulling them back and would have put her feet right on that nightmarish creature.

Crimson came out of the bathroom and said, "It's gone completely."

She couldn't take her eyes off the bed. Crimson turned her until she was looking at him. "I scented with my beast, and there are no other maw-serpents, or any other creatures, in the bedroom. It's perfectly safe."

She wanted to believe him, but the image of the snake lunging at her was burned into her brain.

"Do those things come inside houses often?"

"They're not even from this area."

Something about the look in his eyes told her he had a good idea of how that creepy thing wound up in his bed. "Tell me."

With only a heartbeat of hesitation, he told her about the she-fairy named Giwyn who had been angry when he kicked her out of bed.

"They're not poisonous, but they will ruin your day. Their fangs emit a paralyzing toxin that lasts for several hours." He shook his head. "I can't imagine her being angry enough to do that, and at any rate, no one knows we've mated, so it was directed at me."

"Your friends do, and those women with them at the hot springs."

"Oh." His brow furrowed. Then he shook his head. "I'll cast a protection spell around the house to make sure no one else can get into the house except you and me."

She agreed that it was a good idea. Then she said, "How did you do that sword thing?"

He smiled. "I manifested it."

"That was pretty awesome."

"Yeah?" His chest puffed up a bit with pride, and she grinned as she nodded.

"Can you do me a favor?" She looked up into his eyes.

"Anything."

"Would it be okay if we didn't sleep in the bedroom tonight?"

The humor faded from his eyes quickly, replaced by gentle concern. Stroking his thumb down her cheek, he said, "I don't have another bed, but we can sleep on the sofa."

He kissed her.

"Thank you."

"You don't have to thank me for making you happy or keeping you safe. I nearly blew it. I won't take your safety for granted again."

He swung her up into his arms and carried her into the front room, depositing her on the comfortable sofa before walking back into the bedroom. A few minutes later, he returned with their drinks, and they sat together on the sofa, talking until their stomachs rumbled for dinner.

Even though they'd been interrupted and the mood had been shattered, she was glad to have the chance to get to know more about him. She just hoped no more snakes made any bedroom appearances and that the psycho fairy who'd planted the thing in the bed would take a hint and leave them alone.

Chapter Twelve

After casting the protection spell over his home, he fixed dinner for Lindy then portal-called Riyad. "A maw-serpent? Man, that Giwyn is one vindictive bitch."

"No kidding. I don't know for sure it was her, but my instincts tell me that it was. Would you do me a favor?"

"Name it."

"I put a spell on the house, but I was hoping you'd be willing to keep tabs on Giwyn for a few days."

Riyad rolled his eyes. "Oh yeah, it'll be a real hardship to spy on a beautiful redhead."

Crimson hadn't thought she was all that pretty, but Riyad had a thing for redheads. "She may have put a maw-serpent in my bed. You really want to tangle with her?"

"Maybe she's just crazy from not enough sex. It happens, you know." Riyad shrugged.

"Your funeral. And thanks."

"I'll keep you posted. Go take care of your mate. I got this covered."

The call ended, and he turned to look at Lindy who was standing at the back door, looking out into the yard. He desperately wanted to go back to when they were about to make love. His body was still humming from the kiss and the way her body had smelled when she was aroused. But he wasn't going to make love to her for the first time on the sofa. It just didn't feel right. No, his sweetheart deserved to be treated like a queen, and that meant not taking advantage of things and really making her feel cared for.

He joined her at the door, placing his hands on her hips. "Are you looking at the scenery or thinking?"

"A bit of both, I guess." After a short pause she said, "It's really beautiful here. It's like my realm, but without the modern touches. Instead of power lines crisscrossing the skies, tall buildings, and traffic noises, there are enormous trees, houses carved from stone, and birds and small animals chattering away."

"Our realms are very different," he mused, not only to her but also to himself.

She looked up at him. "Could you be happy away from here? If we would choose to live in my realm?"

Before she had come into his life, he wouldn't have been happy anywhere but where he was. Now, however, nothing was as important to him as making her happy and being with her, and where they chose to live wasn't as important as the fact that they would be together.

He pressed a kiss to her forehead. "Wherever you are is going to be home for me, Lindy. It's as simple as that. If we decide to live here or there, then it's a decision we'll arrive at together. And nothing has to be set in stone. Your realm is a portal-call away."

She looked back over the yard. "Will your parents be okay with you mating a Were from the Mortal Realm?"

That reminded him that he hadn't shared his history with her yet. And he would. In the morning.

"My father already knew that I was spelling for you, and I told him what happened after I found you. He'll like you because you're my mate and that makes you part of our family. My mother doesn't know about you yet because she's off on a spa trip."

He felt her body tense slightly, and he frowned, drawing her closer. "My mother would have liked for me to mate with a she-fairy of high status among our people because she's very interested in bettering her own station. She never asked me what I wanted, though."

He turned her to face him and captured her hands with his. "If she had asked me, I would have told her that I wanted to find the one woman who's perfect for me and that it didn't matter a bit whether she was fae or human or any other type of supernatural creature."

Lindy smiled. "I believe my mom will be happy I've found someone. She's spent her whole life looking for her truemate."

He was glad she was so confident in her mother's reaction to their mating. It hadn't occurred to him that her family might not like him because he was worried about how his mother would react. It really didn't matter if her mother didn't like him, or his mother didn't like her, because they were truemates, and that meant forever.

He smiled. "It's been a long day. Ready for bed?"

Her eyes darted to the sofa, and she smiled. "Yep."

Normally one to sleep nude, he chose to take off only his shirt and remain in his leather trousers. They weren't the most comfortable pants, but he didn't want her to see how turned on he was just being in her presence. She might want to touch him, and he might want to let her, and then his plans to romance and seduce her would go flying out the window as he pinned her to the sofa and had his way with her. Not that it would be a bad thing, necessarily, because his wolf was howling that it was a very excellent thing. But it wasn't romantic. He wanted to show his mate he would respect her in every way and that he was different from any other males she'd known.

He settled on his back on the hide-covered sofa and put his head on a pillow. She stretched out next to him, and he pulled her close so her head rested on his shoulder. After saying goodnight, he willed the lights off and fell asleep.

———•———

By the time Lindy woke in the morning, he had showered and dressed, picked flowers from the garden, placed them in a vase on the kitchen table, and prepared a casserole of *cerion* eggs, goat cheese, and *pash* meat. She sat up from the sofa with a yawn, stretching her arms up. Sleeping with her in his arms for the second night had been amazing. He'd never slept so peacefully.

After kissing her good morning, he sent her off to shower while the casserole cooked and he set the table.

She came into the kitchen a while later with her pretty blonde hair tied back in a braid and wearing a white dress with yellow flowers on it. She looked fresh and lovely, and pride filled him at her beauty.

After pulling her chair out and tucking her close to the table, he served her a wedge of casserole and fresh juice then sat down across from her. All morning while he prepared the meal for her, he had been thinking about his life and what he was going to share with her. He'd never told anyone *everything* about himself before. His friends and family knew him well, but no one knew all of his secrets. He was glad to be sharing his life with Lindy and that she would be the only woman to know every part of him.

As they ate, he began to tell her about his life. Crimson's real father—his biological father—was a werewolf from the Mortal Realm who had fallen in love with his mother when they were both quite young. She became pregnant, and before they could be mated officially, he had been killed by hunters on the full moon.

"My biological father was best friends with a fae named Desmin. At the time, the fae council had a liaison office in the Mortal Realm, and that's where my biological father and Desmin became close. They both loved my mom, and when my biological father died, Desmin stepped in to support my mom and claimed me as his own. I know he's not my biological father, but he's the only one I've ever known."

When he was born, his eyes had been red, which is what prompted his parents to name him Crimson. His eyes faded to green within a month, but they didn't realize that the red eyes were an indication that he was a *wulfen*. Most fae learned how to control their wings when they were between the ages of five and eight. He was three when he first made his wings unfurl from his back, and his parents took it as a sign that he was going to be a strong fae-warrior for his people. His training had begun early, and he learned how to fight and handle many weapons from the best teachers in the realm. As he grew older, he began to grow restless.

"I always felt like something was wrong with me. I wanted to race into the woods and hunt with my bare hands. I wanted to yell at the sky when the moon was full. And I was so horny on the nights of the full moon when I was a teenager that I got a reputation for being a *vauslav*."

"*Vauslav?*" she asked.

"I think you would say I was a player."

She nodded in understanding. "You just wanted sex."

"Yeah. I didn't understand at the time, but I believe now that the reason I never wanted any long-term relationships was because the females weren't my truemate. When I was sixteen, I shifted into my wolf form for the first time, and it was the singularly most terrifying thing that ever happened to me. I thought I was dying. I was with my best friend, Riyad, and we were hanging out at the hot springs. It was a full moon, and we were entertaining some she-fairies and hoping to score." His cheeks blushed as he said the words, but she'd been open with him, and he was going to be open with her, too. "Then my joints started to crack, and my skin prickled like needles were trying to push through my flesh. The first shift took hours, and I screamed myself hoarse. Riyad called for a healer to come help me, and he recognized immediately that I was a *wulfen* and trying to shift. He told me not to fight it, but I was so scared that I couldn't relax and let the change come."

She reached across the table and clasped his hand. "Even growing up with wolves, the first time is traumatic. It got better after that?"

He nodded. "I was still a nervous wreck the next month, but it was easier. *Wulfen* are legendary among my people."

Desmin was a decorated veteran in the fae military and served for many years. Even before Crimson shifted for the first time, he knew he would follow in his father's footsteps. He joined the military at seventeen and quickly rose up through the ranks because of his training. The military considered it a boon that they had a *wulfen* in their midst.

"This is the Fae Realm, but that doesn't mean that everyone within this realm is fae. The military handles everything from full-scale wars to private matters the way your human police force would. One day I might be handling a robbery in the market and the next day I might be clashing swords with a wizard. There are shifters here that aren't like anything in your realm, and just like in your realm, there are evil people who want to do harm for their own personal gain."

She stroked her thumb across the top of his hand. "I grew up hearing stories about tiny little fairies who hid in flowers and made clothes out of leaves. Your world is nothing like I believed."

He was certain that was true of most people from her realm. He continued on in his life's story, telling her about his mother's insistence that he spend time with high-bred females and go to all the parties. She'd hoped he would want to settle down with a female who came from a family that would get her access to a world she'd not had access to because her family, and his father's family, were not part of the wealthy elite.

When their meal was done and the dishes washed and put away, he continued his story as they walked toward the center of town. He hadn't really realized how dissatisfied he'd been with his life – just going through the motions – until she'd come into it. Just two days with her and already he felt more alive, and definitely happier.

They came to the center of town, and he showed her the tavern where he and the other members of the military came to unwind, the market where vendors hocked their food and wares, and the courthouse where civil and criminal matters were handled.

She held his hand tightly as they walked. They passed many fae along the way, with everyone greeting her warmly, and he could see she was relieved. He could tell she wanted to be accepted in his world, and he could admit to feeling the same concern when he considered being in her world. He wanted her friends and pack to accept him, too.

"Do you have prison here?" she asked when he took her into one of the glen's public gardens. Towering *flinks* flowers waved gently in the breeze, their honey-like scent filling the air.

She sat down on a marble bench, and he joined her. "We do. Our judicial system is not all that different from the Mortal Realm's courts. Here, trials are presided over by fae judges, and sentences for crimes vary from monetary fines to community service to imprisonment."

"Ever been in trouble?" she asked, looking at him out of the corner of her eye with a mischievous smile.

He hummed in his throat. "When I was twelve, Riyad and I thought it would be fun to sneak onto a *grent* farm. They're hens that have silky bright blue feathers. Some girls from school said that if we would bring them the feathers, they would spend time with us."

Lindy chuckled.

He continued, "Anyway, what we didn't know was that while *grents* look very docile they've actually got really sharp beaks and spikes along their clawed feet. And they're extremely protective of their eggs. Riyad and I thought the *grents* were sleeping, but when we touched their long tail feathers, they attacked us. Suffice it to say we barely made it out of their coop with our bodies intact."

She laughed and said, "Did you at least get feathers to give to the girls?"

He shook his head. "We're lucky we didn't lose any fingers. And it turns out that Riyad is really allergic to *grent* feathers, and he had to see a healer to stop from sneezing constantly."

"So you had to see a judge?"

"Yes. The *grents* were so stressed out that a few of them died, and the farmer did a location spell to find out who had broken into the coop. We had to publically apologize to the farmer, fix the door of the coop that we'd broken, clean up the mess we made, and pay to replace the *grents* that died."

"Wow. I bet you never did anything like that again."

"True. My dad was very understanding and just wanted me to learn from my mistake, but my mother was horrified the prank would somehow reflect poorly on her mothering abilities."

He said the words lightly, but suddenly he didn't feel so pleased to be sharing that story. Yes, it was funny, but at the moment, it just reminded him of how worried his mother had always been about her social standing.

"Hey," she said softly, turning his chin with her fingers. "If your mother isn't proud of you, then she's blind. I've never met anyone like you before, Crimson. You're brave and strong. You're gorgeous and funny and kind."

He pressed his lips to her palm. "And really lucky."

"I'm lucky, too."

Her smile made his insides warm.

"Do you think your mom will like me?" he asked, taking her hand and standing. They began to walk back through the market.

"I'm sure she will. What's not to like? Besides the fact that you're my truemate, you saved my life."

They stopped at a market stall selling dresses, and he told her to pick out something for when they went to dinner with his father the following evening. As she looked through the dresses of varying lengths and hues, he said, "It seems like it's simpler with your people than mine."

"What...acceptance?" She held up a dress the color of lilacs.

"Yes. Your pack doesn't have social standing the way that my people do. It's refreshing."

She put the purple dress back and pulled a teal one down, which he thought would look amazing with her pretty blue eyes.

"There's a hierarchy within the pack. The males are ranked during rank-fights, which only occur at times when a member leaves the pack for some reason or if a member becomes unable to perform the duties of his rank. The higher the rank, the more responsibilities there are."

He paid for the dress, and they watched as it was wrapped up in colorful fabric and tied with ribbon. "And the females?"

"Before the current alpha, the females were ranked after rank-fights as well. When I came into my shifted form at sixteen, I trained with some of the older females for a while and then fought for my place. At the time, there were a few females who were very good fighters, and I wound up mid-ranked. Those females left for one reason or another, and then for many years there was no female alpha. Cadence took over a couple years ago, but she never held new rank-fights, so the old ranking has stood."

"How many females are there?"

"There are only thirteen active she-wolves in the pack. Males and females will technically 'retire' from the pack as they age and no longer participate in rankings, so there are a lot of wolves in town, but our pack only has around forty active members. There are a lot of young wolves who haven't shifted yet, too. In the next couple of years there will be a population explosion within the pack, and Cades will have no choice but to hold ranking fights to be fair to everyone."

He held her hand as they walked back to his home. "You'd like to be higher ranked?"

"Not necessarily. What I do regret is that I alienated myself from the pack for such a long time. I became a virtual stranger, just someone who shows up on the full moons and goes hunting with her best friends. I've been working to change that, to change myself into someone I'm proud of. When I was younger, I wanted to fit in, and I thought I could do that by being like my mom. I always thought she was so popular. She dated all the time when I was little; there were always men showing up at the house to talk to her. Then I found myself in that same place, but where she'd embraced it and taken all those failed dates as stepping stones to finding her mate, I just felt used. And then I hated myself for trying to fit in."

He held open the door to his home and ushered her inside. "You fit in with me, Lindy."

She turned to him with a brilliant smile, her eyes dancing with happiness. "You fit in with me, too."

While they'd been out walking, he had an idea for their mating night. Although he had changed the sheets on the bed and the protection spell kept out any unwanted visitors, he felt as if that room had been tainted. He didn't want the first time he and Lindy made love to be in that room, on the bed that Giwyn and countless other women had been naked on. He'd told her that her past didn't matter to him, and that was true. But his own past – the random females, the meaningless sex – filled him with shame. After knowing how powerful their connection already was, he knew he wouldn't trade one of her sweet kisses for all the fae pussy in the realm, and he wished, in some ways, that he'd saved himself for her.

She'd been tired after they spent the morning walking around the realm, so he lay next to her on the couch and stroked her back with his hands until she fell asleep. While she slept, he began to make preparations for their night. He'd told her that he wanted to make her his mate in a ceremony in the traditions of the *old ways*, which had gotten him to thinking about how he could make their first night together special and unique. He wanted to make love to her for the first time and be able to honestly say that he'd never done anything like it before with anyone else. The ceremonial old ways, referring to the official mating between the fae warriors and their brides, was not about sex but about joining them together in front of the realm. He wanted to do that and would talk to his father the following night about it. But this night – when he and Lindy would mate and mark each other – was going to be a night where he could show her just how special she was to him. She was already the center of his world. He'd never known affection for a female like this before, and he knew he was fast falling in love with her.

After making a portal-call to Riyad, he filled a large satchel with supplies and left his sleeping sweetheart on the couch with a note in case she awoke. He let his wings loose and flew to the place where he and his friends used to play as youngsters, a cavern in the nearby mountains. Inside the cavern was a hot spring. Riyad was waiting for him, a smile on his face.

Riyad clapped him on the shoulder. "I'm happy you've found your mate, Crim, and glad to help."

Crimson appreciated his best friend and thanked him. They ducked inside the low entrance to the cavern, which widened immediately and was tall enough for them to stand up. The entrance spilled out into the rounded cavern, and he inhaled deeply, checking with his wolf's instincts for anything that might not be welcome. Finding the cavern clear of creatures, he pulled a torch from his satchel and willed it to light, setting it in an alcove near the entrance. The cavern had natural vents in the high ceiling that allowed smoke and steam from the hot spring to escape.

Crimson shared his plan with Riyad on how he wanted to alter the cavern for his mating night, and Riyad got to work while Crimson turned his attention to lighting more torches and setting them in alcoves to provide subtle lighting. When the torches had been placed, he moved to the center of the cavern where a ring of stones was filled with purple *colaras*, also known as fire stones. They were mined on the other side of the realm, and he'd brought them to the cavern when they were children so they would have light and warmth when they played without having to use wood.

Although he, Riyad, and Merik had spent a lot of time in the cavern, exploring the mountainside and tunnels, none of them had ever brought females. He remembered that Riyad's grandfather had told them about the caverns and tunnels dotting the mountainside, sharing how warriors of old had stolen females and hidden them away to be pleasured until they agreed to officially mate the warriors. Riyad's grandfather had stolen his grandmother while she was walking home from a party and kept her in a cavern for a week until she agreed to be his mate. Now, he wasn't kidnapping Lindy but bringing her willingly to a place where no other woman had ever been in his arms and he could worship her and make love to her in the way of his ancestors. And then, later, he would stand up in front of his people and make her his mate, and no one would ever dare try to take her from him.

No one had been in the cavern for years. The fire stones were covered with a thick layer of dust and cobwebs, which disintegrated when he used his power to light them. Although purple in color, once lit, the stones changed colors, some red, some blue, some green. They warmed immediately, and he smiled. Lindy would like them. She thought his fae power was *resh*.

"Cool," he amended out loud.

"What's cool?" Riyad asked.

"Lindy says 'cool' when she means *resh*. I was just thinking that she would think the fire stones were cool."

Riyad said, "Help me spread *balnk* seeds around the pool."

Crimson stood and joined his friend at the hot spring, a pool of steaming water that was five feet deep at the center and fed from a small waterfall along the wall of the cavern. He and Riyad spread dark green *balnk* seeds around the perimeter of the pool, and then they stepped back and Riyad lifted his hands, calling the seeds to life. Dark green blades of grass sprang from the seeds, spreading across the cavern floor. Riyad stopped the flow of grass when it had covered half of the cavern in thick, silky grass. The grass was hardy and could take root in stone, which is why Riyad had suggested it when Crimson laid out his idea. He couldn't give Lindy a carpeted cavern, but he could make a carpet of grass for her.

"What do you think of the mattress?" Riyad asked, and Crimson turned to look at the task his friend had completed. Crimson hadn't been able to carry an entire bed up the mountain, and he didn't want to just lay his mate on the hard stone. Riyad had caused moss seeds to grow, shaping them into a thick mattress. Sitting down on the moss, Crimson was amazed that it felt exactly like his comfortable mattress at home.

He ran his hands over the soft moss. "This is amazing."

"Aw, thanks. I'm glad you like it. At least you're not going to be lying on blankets on the stone floor. Even with the *balnk* grass, it would still be uncomfortable." Riyad took four small tree limbs and moved around the mattress, sticking one into the moss at each corner. As Crimson watched, Riyad used his power to make the limbs grow. Each limb had been no thicker than the width of his finger, but the tiny branches on the limbs twisted and grew, forming a thick braid of branches that rose several feet in the air at each corner of the moss bed. With a push of power from Riyad, who grunted slightly with exertion, the limbs connected overhead in the center of the bed, leaves and branches forming a canopy overtop of the mattress.

Riyad reached up and placed a little green vine on one branch and filled it with power. The vine grew quickly, twining between the branches and then sprouting tiny pink flowers, covering the entire underside of the canopy.

Leaning back on his elbows, Crimson looked up, admiring his friend's handiwork. "Wow." Raising a brow at Riyad, he said, "You're pretty romantic. I had no idea."

Riyad blushed and scuffed at the cavern floor with the toe of his boot. "Just don't go telling everyone. I'll have every male in the glen wanting me to help them impress their mate."

Getting up, Crimson laid a soft sheet across the moss then placed two pillows at the head of the bed and folded a blanket at the foot of the bed. He left the food and drink in the satchel and tucked it against one wall then surveyed their work. Riyad's power had turned the stark, manly cavern into a beautiful oasis. Crimson knew that he could bring Lindy here and what they would share would be the start of their new life together.

He clapped his best friend on the back and thanked him for his help. Sealing the cavern door with a protection spell, Crimson flew off toward home and Riyad headed off in another direction. He would have to remember to send Riyad a proper thank you for his assistance.

As he walked into his home, he saw that Lindy was still asleep. He crumpled up the note and joined her on the couch, curling her warm body against him and breathing in the sweet scent of his mate.

Chapter Thirteen

After Lindy woke from her nap, Crimson told her he was taking her for an overnight trip to a very special place. She'd wanted to ask for more details, but judging from the heated look in his green eyes, she knew that no matter where it was, they were going to be mated by morning.

He'd promised to seduce her, and he had. When he'd first said he would seduce her, she'd expected a full-blown physical assault meant to weaken her emotional defenses. Crimson had done the opposite. He'd seduced her mentally and emotionally, and not in the way she'd anticipated. Simply by accepting her and taking his time with her, he'd proven himself to be much different than any other male she'd known. And more than the seduction was the fact that he'd saved her life. He'd come through the portal and brought her back without hesitation and offered her everything he had.

She was quickly falling in love with her handsome *wulfen*, and it was both the most terrifying and freeing things she'd ever done.

He had packed a small bag for her, and after she changed into shorts, a short-sleeved shirt, and tennis shoes, he took her hand and walked out of the house. He hooked the bag over his shoulder, tightening it so it lay flush to his bare chest.

He turned and exhaled, his wings slipping from his back silently. He stretched them out and then picked up her hand. "Ready for a ride?"

"Really?" She looked up at the blue sky and then at his wings.

"It would be a long walk to get to our destination, but we can get there in less than an hour by flight."

He turned and went down on one knee in front of her, looking over his shoulder at her expectantly.

"Are you sure you can carry me that far?"

He rolled his eyes with a smile. "You're my mate. I wouldn't risk your safety if I didn't know for a fact that it will be no burden to carry you."

She climbed onto his back. He hooked her knees with his arms as she wrapped her arms around his neck. He asked if she was ready, and she said that she was, nerves skating through her as his wings flapped, and they lifted off the ground. The air rushed around them, and she glanced down then closed her eyes with a shaky breath, leaning her head against his shoulder.

He squeezed her legs with his arms. "You okay, *chelle*?"

She opened her eyes and looked out at the blue sky. She felt the muscles in his back working as his wings moved. She exhaled slowly and felt her body relax against him. She trusted him more than she'd ever trusted anyone.

Kissing the back of his neck, she said, "I'm great."

While they flew, he told her about the glens, which were the fae-realms' version of cities. It surprised her to learn how similar the glens were to her realms' cities, separated by class, which for fae was attributed to their power. There were blue-collar powers and white-collar powers, ruling class and working class.

"What are warriors?" she asked, watching the homes pass by below them as they soared through the air.

"Upper class, but not elite. The elite are the ruling class. The upper class includes warriors and fae with powers like my friend Riyad who controls plant life, and his brother, Merik, who can control water."

"They're brothers but don't have the same powers?"

"Riyad takes after his mother, and Merik after his father. My mom can control fire, which is a noble power."

"Noble?"

He paused for a moment and said, "Respected, I guess is the term to use. There are powers that are necessary but not respected, workers that use their hands along with their powers. Such as *lock-infae*, like the fairy female in your pack. Her ability to manipulate metals is not considered a noble power."

"I don't understand why one power is better than another. I think any kind of power is pretty cool."

"I guess when everyone has powers, it's natural to segregate according to those powers. Elemental powers – air, earth, fire, water – are noble and respected powers. Other powers are non-noble and those who wield them are considered lower class."

"So the popular kids in your school were the ones like you who could control the elements?"

"Pretty much."

"And your mom wants you to mate with a female fairy that can also control an element."

He snorted in annoyance. "Yes. But that doesn't matter. In time she'll accept our mating, especially when she gets to know you and sees how wonderful you are and how right we are for each other."

She appreciated his vote of confidence, but she wasn't so sure. His mom sounded like she wouldn't be accepting of anyone other than a noble fae female as a mate for her son.

"Hey," Crimson said, squeezing one knee as he began to take them lower in the sky, "don't get down on yourself, Lindy. You're beautiful and sweet and kind. And you're mine, and that's all that matters to me."

"It's all that matters to me, too."

A mountain range stretched beneath them, and Crimson flew in lazy circles, bringing them lower and lower. She saw caves interspersed along the face of the mountain and was surprised when Crimson landed on a ledge in front of one cavern. He spoke a few words she didn't know, and the air in front of the entrance to the cave seemed to shimmer then clear. She recognized it as a protection spell like the one he used around his home.

He went to one knee, and she climbed off, turning to look back at the glens they had passed over on their way to the mountains. Crimson dropped his pack to the ground and moved behind her, putting his arms around her. He explained that the mountains were known as Hades Ridge.

Underneath their feet, a small trail was carved into the rock and headed down the mountainside. She didn't know how far up they were, but she was fairly sure that a fall from this height would ruin her day. Woods and grassy fields spread out in front of them, and the glen that Crimson said was called the Winnower Glen was visible.

He scooped her up in his arms, snagged the bag from the ground, and carried her inside the cavern. Once inside, he straightened and spoke a spell, and the entrance of the cave shimmered again then cleared. He had told her back at his home that no one could get through the protection spell, not even animals or birds. They could leave while the protection spell was up, but although Crimson could enter without removing the spell, she couldn't. She thought the protection spell seemed like the best security system ever, but Crimson told her it required power to call the spell, and it would be impossible for even the most powerful fae to keep the protection spell up forever.

He kissed her, and when the kiss broke, she was aware of flickering light around them. Looking over her shoulder, she gasped in shock at the cavern. The walls of the cave were smooth stone, and the high ceiling had what appeared to be vents in it. Along the dark walls were torches she knew Crimson had lit. In the center of the room was a pile of colorful, glowing stones that flickered as if flames were captured inside.

She could see what looked like green carpet in front of a giant steaming pool against one wall. Crimson carried her across the stone floor to an enormous canopy bed that appeared to be made out of woven branches. He sat her down on the end of the bed, bent, and placed a kiss on her forehead. Wordlessly, he left her and carried the bag to a corner where he pulled another, larger bag out and began to rummage inside. She leaned back on her elbows and looked up at the woven canopy above her. Delicate pink flowers on a narrow green vine wove through the interlaced branches. They smelled sweet and looked amazing, like little pink stars in a green sky.

Crimson appeared in front of her with two wooden cups. He sat next to her, and they turned to face each other as he handed her one cup. She sniffed at the dark liquid inside the cup and thought it smelled faintly like peach wine she'd had once.

"Centuries ago," he said as he looked down at the cup, "a warrior fae would see a female that he wanted to mate with, and he would capture her and bring her up to a cavern. He would pleasure her until she agreed to mate with him, and then he would take her home, and they would join in front of their family and friends." He lifted his eyes and smiled at her. "I know I don't have to kidnap you, Lindy, because you know that you're mine and I'm yours, but I want to do everything the way that my ancestors did. One of the things they did with their intended was share a drink of *nasale*, a wine made of *goju berries* and *citri flowers*. It's said to encourage a long and happy mating."

He touched their cups together and said, "To us. I'm so glad you're my mate."

She said, "I'm so glad you're mine, too."

Lifting the cup to her lips, she drank the sweet liquid, relishing the knowledge that she and Crimson would be mated by morning and that nothing would keep them apart.

With their cups drained, Crimson took them and set them on the floor and then cupped her face with his warm hands. He pressed his lips to hers, just once, and pulled away slightly.

"Say you're mine," he growled lightly, and she answered, "Always," before he crashed against her mouth with a throaty growl and wrapped his arms around her. His tongue slid against hers. The taste of the wine and the heady, masculine flavor of him filled her. Her hands gripped his shoulders as he slid his tongue against hers in a dance that so closely mimicked sex she felt as if she was on the verge of coming from that alone. His lips moved sensually, softly, a counterpoint to the aggressive thrust of his tongue, driving her wild.

He left her mouth, and she gasped for air as he tipped her face up, nipping at her chin and throat. Her fingers slipped down the front of his chest, her thumbs rubbing his nipples before tracing the ridges of his abdomen. Peeling her top off, he cupped her breasts and lifted them, nuzzling his lips against the lace-covered mounds.

With some effort, she abandoned her exploration of his body and undid her bra. He tugged it off, and she stretched out on her back, lifting her arms and beckoning him forward. He stretched out on his side next to her and kissed her as his hand touched her breasts, stroking and teasing her nipples. Her hands fisted in his hair as he left her mouth and plumped her breast, sucking her nipple deeply into his mouth. Her back arched as pleasure shot through her. He sucked and licked her nipples, alternating between them until they were tight, hot peaks and her body was humming with pleasure.

The button of her shorts opened, and the zipper slipped down as Crimson moved down the bed, tugging her shorts and panties down her hips. After discarding her shoes and socks, he stripped her completely then divested himself of his own clothes before kneeling between her legs. He pushed her thighs apart and gazed down at her pussy. She lay before him, stripped bare both physically and emotionally, and felt herself fall in love with him a little bit more. He leaned forward and inhaled over her pussy. A possessive growl trickled from his throat. He gazed up at her, his eyes bleeding from green to red. "Mine."

It had never felt so right to be claimed. "Yours."

He licked his lips and seemed to wrestle with his control for a moment. His eyes bled back to green, but his voice retained a harsh edge. "Once I taste you, *chelle*, I'm not going to stop until you're wearing my marks on your neck and my come has filled your sweet pussy. I want you forever, and I won't take anything less."

She cast the last of her worries away and nodded. "I'm yours forever, Crimson, and I want you to be mine, too."

"I was yours the moment I picked you up into my arms in your realm, Lindy. Heart, soul, life. Everything I am or ever will be is yours."

He stared at her for a heartbeat longer and then stroked the flat of his tongue across her clit. Pleasure trembled through her at the simple movement. He licked her again, his tongue twirling around her clit with slow, deliberate movements. Then he cupped her bottom and lifted her lower body off the bed. He tilted his head to the side and speared her pussy with his tongue, growling as he stroked inside her. The growls made his tongue vibrate, and she gasped as he licked her deeply, his tongue stroking and vibrating with his hungry growls. He circled the entrance of her pussy and then flicked his tongue rapidly over her clit. Her legs trembled, and her stomach clenched as she gripped the blanket underneath her.

He sucked her clit into his mouth, his lips closing around the sensitive bud as his tongue swirled around it, and she reached for him, fisting his hair and pulling him hard to her body. Heat filled her, and she cried out his name as she came, grinding her pussy against his mouth as he left her clit and fucked her with his tongue, lapping at her cream like a contented cat.

He growled as he laid her body gently on the mattress. His fingers slipped over her hips, and he seemed to be wrestling with something. She looked down the length of her body and saw his cock twitching. His body was tense, and his muscles were tight and straining.

"Crimson?" she whispered.

"Want to," his voice was low and laced with need, "face you but need to take you."

It took only a second for her to figure out the meaning of his growled words. His beast wanted to dominate her, but his fae side wanted to make love to her, face to face. She wiggled out of his hold and rolled onto her stomach. She went to her knees and spread her legs apart. She gathered her hair to one side to bare her neck to him, and it was all the invitation he needed. He covered her body with his, his hard cock thrusting into her as he held her with one arm banded around her waist. His other hand was planted next to hers, his fingers digging into the blanket as he pulled out of her and shoved back in. He held her so tight she couldn't move, taking her hard and fast.

Her body soared with pleasure that coiled tighter and tighter inside her. She moaned and tried to move, but he snarled and bit down on the place where her neck and shoulder met. Sharp fangs pierced her skin, and she gasped as the pain faded to a warm throb. He gripped her tighter around the waist, angling her hips up farther until she cried out as his cock hit a place deep inside her. She gasped out halting breaths as he pounded into her, rubbing that spot over and over as he growled into her shoulder. Swamped with pleasure, overwhelmed with sensation, she gave herself up to him.

Her orgasm flashed through her like lightning, branding her body and soul. He came, lifting his mouth from her shoulder, his howl splitting the silence of the cavern as his cock spasmed deep inside her. Her pussy locked down on his cock as the pleasure flowed over her like a waterfall, warming her from head to toe.

"Crimson, Crimson," she moaned his name as he held her tight.

"Lindy," he groaned and eased his body from hers. The pull of his cock from her sensitive pussy made her shiver, and he settled on his side and pulled her into his arms. His tongue stroked over the mark he'd made on her shoulder.

Possessive feelings stole over her, and she twisted in his arms and flattened him on his back, caging him with her arms. She knew he could easily best her; he was stronger than her and gifted with fae abilities as well as his supernatural shifter genes. That he willingly let her dominate him now erased some of the inadequacy she'd felt since she'd met him. He really was her mate, because only a male who was mated to a female would allow himself to be taken to his back and marked.

Her fangs elongated at the thought of marking him, and his eyes, which were still red, sought hers for a moment before he bared his neck to her. She growled his name and sank her fangs into the side of his neck. Her pack normally marked on the back of the neck over the spine, but she and her wolf both wanted his marks to be visible to everyone at all times. The sweet tang of his blood crested her tongue as his arms wrapped around her and held her close.

"Yes," he hissed, molding her body to his, one hand moving into her hair and holding her head in place.

Releasing the hold on his neck, she licked the edges of her fangs before they receded into her mouth. She stroked her tongue over the marks.

Their eyes met once more and they both spoke at the same time. "Mine."

Chapter Fourteen

Lindy snuggled close to him, and his wolf howled in triumph at the slight pain in his neck from where her delicate fangs had pierced him. The marks were healing, scarring over so that they would remain for the rest of his life as proof that he and Lindy were mated. He had loved sinking his fangs into her neck, too, and judging by the way her pussy had spasmed in climax again, he knew that she enjoyed it, too.

He was falling in love with her. All the years of wondering where he fit in, and it turned out he fit perfectly with this wolf shifter from the mortal realm.

After their hearts stopped pounding, he picked her up and carried her over to the hot spring. He put her down on the grass, and she wiggled her toes saying, "I thought it was carpet!"

"Riyad helped me prepare the cave for you. I wanted this to be as comfortable as I could make it."

"It's all so beautiful."

Yes, she was.

He retrieved two towels and a bottle of bathing oil from one of the packs and placed them at the edge of the pool. He stepped down onto the first step. The almost-too-hot water covered his feet. He reached for her hands, and she followed willingly as he moved down each step, pausing for long moments as their bodies adjusted to the temperature of the water. When they had both dunked under the water, he led her to a depression carved into the pool where she could recline against the side.

Using the bathing oil, he massaged the sweet-smelling liquid into her skin, one of the rituals from his ancestors. As he lifted one leg out of the water, he planted her foot on his chest and massaged her calf, explaining that fae males used scent in their bonding rituals. He had chosen honeysuckle oil because he knew she liked the aroma of the soap in his home, and he found that it reminded him of her naturally sweet scent. If a female was particularly disagreeable to mating, a male might use flowers that promoted relaxation.

She cocked a brow at him. "Your ancestors used flowers to drug women into mating with them?"

He chuckled and massaged her foot. "That's one way of looking at it. A male would never take a female against her will. He might kidnap her and keep her in seclusion, but he would have been certain that she was meant for him before he began his seduction." Returning her foot to the water, he lifted her other foot. "How am I doing so far?"

"I'm thoroughly seduced." Her eyelids fluttered shut as he worked on her leg, and he grinned. Nothing about casting the truemate spell had gone the way he thought it would, but he couldn't be happier.

"Do all fae cast the truemate spells?"

"No. Normally, if a fae hasn't found his mate by the time he or she reaches twenty-five, they'll cast the truemate spell. It's considered strange for a male or female not to cast the spell in their twenty-fifth year."

"So you not doing it was weird?"

He nodded. "Because I had no plans to cast the spell, my mom sent females to me, hoping one of them would end up being my mate. A fae mother can choose her son's mate if she feels he's neglecting his duty to mate and bear young."

"Like an arranged marriage?"

"Something like that. But she didn't ask me what I wanted, or she would have known that I wanted the female meant to belong to me and my wolf."

She hummed in her throat. "I think in the old days, wolves traveled a lot more, looking for their truemates. But now, wolves will settle down with someone they love regardless of whether that person is their truemate or not."

He frowned. "Sounds like the wolf wouldn't care for that."

"I've heard that the wolves will never feel truly content, but they will settle into the mating eventually. I think," she paused for only a moment, "I think that I would have done that if someone had actually wanted me. I would have settled into a mating that wasn't right for me just because I thought it was what I needed. It scares me to think about what might have been, what I would have lost out on."

"I could have accepted one of the females my mother sent for me and settled, too. In a way I'm grateful that she pushed me so often because it made me willing to take my future into my own hands."

"Why didn't you spell for me when you turned twenty-five?"

"I was so wrapped up in being the best soldier I could be, following in my dad's footsteps, that I didn't think I had time for a mating. I didn't care about my personal life. I just wanted my career to be as amazing as my dad's. He reminded me that the only way I could get my mom to stop trying to choose my mate was to spell for her myself. I felt like I needed to wait until the full moon to do it. I don't know why."

"Maybe your wolf knew I would need you."

"If I hadn't waited, though, you wouldn't have gotten hurt."

She smiled, and it made his heart clench. "I've already forgotten everything but waking up to your gorgeous face."

A blush crept into his cheeks and she chuckled at his embarrassment. It pleased him that his mate thought he was handsome, but he wasn't used to being on the receiving end of such praise. He had accolades for his skill in battle, but somehow, knowing that she liked how he looked made all that seem unimportant.

After he had covered every bit of her creamy skin with the oil, they made love on their towels on the grass and then ate the meal he had brought in front of the fire stones. As the sky darkened outside the cave, they made love again on the bed and drifted off to sleep, secure in each other's arms.

In the morning, Lindy straightened outside the cave and looked wistfully back inside. "I really loved being here, Crimson. Thank you for sharing it with me."

He felt a pang of sadness at leaving, too. He'd never felt closer to another person than he did to Lindy, and being in the cave's seclusion, he could see why his ancestors had chosen this method of seduction. He'd been wanting to seduce her, but she'd ended up seducing him thoroughly, too. He couldn't imagine ever being apart from her.

He left the protection spell off the cavern and flew them home. To leave the cave protected when he had no idea when they would use it again was a foolish waste of power. The torches and fire stones were out, and the grass and bed would eventually wither and die unless a *blosomfae* like Riyad came to tend to things. He didn't think Riyad would, although he was sure his friend was more of a romantic than he wanted people to believe. While Crimson had grown tired of being a player, Riyad was enjoying himself, and it wasn't for Crimson to say otherwise.

He took Lindy to lunch at the tavern in the glen and introduced her to some of the males who he fought beside. They sat at a small table and both ate *warfarers* pie filled with roasted *grent* and vegetables.

Bront came up and clapped him on the shoulder. "Heard about your mate, Captain, very happy for ya."

"Thank you, Bront." Crimson introduced Lindy to the large male.

Bront said with a wink, "I hope you're planning to retire from the infantry; it'd be a shame to leave such a pretty mate at home."

Crimson grimaced when he saw Lindy look at Bront in confusion. "Retire?"

Bront raised his brows and then said, "Oh, sorry, I thought you knew, miss. Mated males are allowed to step down from the infantry and take less dangerous jobs." He ducked his head, glancing at Crimson in apology, and left quickly.

"I don't understand. You're a warrior. Why wouldn't they want you to still be a warrior?"

"Well..." He poked at the vegetables swimming in the gravy and said, "It's not that I don't want to be in the infantry, *chelle*, it's just that it's a choice that all newly mated males have to make. I told my commander that I wanted to talk to you about it first before I made any decisions. The front lines are dangerous. Before we met, I went up against a huge bird that killed many of my men in a rampage. I've been shot, stabbed, burned, and had a wizard try to kill me with lightning. Mated males have a responsibility first to their mates and children and then in service to their realm. If I stepped down, I'd still be part of the military but in a safer role as a realm guard or possibly a trainer of new recruits."

"Is that what you want?" She looked genuinely curious.

"I knew that when I found my mate my life would change. I don't want to put myself in harm's way when I have you and our future children to take care of."

He explained that realm guards patrolled the streets and borders of the glens, calling in the military when required and handling small issues as they pertained to the safety of the people.

"Is that what you want?" she said.

He raised a brow. "You already asked me that."

"I know, but you didn't answer. Would you be happy as a realm guard? Is that what you want to do for the rest of your life?"

He rolled the question around in his mind and said, "As long as I have you to come home to, I don't really care what my job is. I wouldn't mind patrolling. It's really no different than police in your realm, and being a trainer is an important job, to help shape the future military."

"What if we don't end up staying here in your realm?"

He ate his last bite of pie and put his fork down, reaching across the table to lace his fingers with hers. "Wherever we go, I'll feel the same, *chelle*."

When they returned home, they tumbled into bed for the rest of the afternoon then showered and dressed for dinner. As he expected, she looked incredible in the teal dress he bought for her. Her silky blonde hair hung down her back like a curtain made of gold, and her blue eyes sparkled with happiness.

His father had said he would send a carriage for them, so he was not surprised to see the carriage already waiting for them when he opened the front door to usher Lindy outside. His parents' driver, Laud, stood next to the black carriage and bowed slightly. "It is good to see you again, sir."

"And you, Laud. This is Lindy, my mate."

Lindy greeted Laud, and then Crimson lifted her into the carriage and sat down next to her on the plush bench. With a flick of his wrist, Laud sent the narrow whip into the flanks of his father's ruby-colored stallion, and the carriage pulled away from his home. Lindy was fascinated by the lack of modern things within the realm, and it wasn't the first time that his conscience had panged at how different things would be for her if they chose to live in the Fae Realm. Would she really be happy here, without cars and television and easy contact with her friends and family? Wolves were social creatures by nature—he knew that because he was one—but he wasn't part of a pack because he was the only *wulfen* around. He'd never really thought about how lonely that made him feel because he'd been caught up in being the best warrior he could be. He mostly ignored his wolf, except for the full moons when he was forced to shift and hunt or when it benefited him to use his extra senses. He wondered what it would be like to really belong to a pack.

"...is just awesome."

He shook himself from his thoughts when Lindy squeezed his hand. "I'm sorry, *chelle*, what did you say?"

"I said the realm is just awesome. I had no idea there was even another realm, and I'm actually here with you. My mate." She smiled at him, and it was the smile he loved the best. The one that made her eyes crinkle with happiness.

He kissed her temple. "I'm glad you're here with me."

Laud stopped the carriage, and Crimson stepped out of the carriage and helped Lindy down onto the cobblestone walkway in front of his parents' home. His father had built the grand home for his mother, the sprawling stone building a testament to their station.

Lindy peeked up at Crimson and whispered, "I like *your* house."

"It's yours now, sweetness."

The front door was opened by Juli, the house servant, who bowed deeply as they walked by. "Master is in the kitchen, sir."

"Thank you, Juli." He held Lindy's hand and led her into the house. "My dad isn't much for pomp and circumstance. He's probably eating out of the pot, which would drive my mom batty if she were here."

"Which is why I don't do it when she's home," his dad said, turning from the stove with a spoon full of chopped vegetables that he ate quickly. He put the spoon down on the marble counter and wiped his hands on his trousers. His dad embraced him tightly, patting his back, and then said, "And this must be your mate, Lindy. How lovely you are."

"It's nice to meet you, sir."

"Sir? Are you mad? Call me Dad."

"All right," Lindy laughed, "Dad."

"That's better. You're truemates, and that means we're family. No pretense here."

They ate at the table in the kitchen, and his dad regaled Lindy with tales of his exploits in various wars and some of Crimson's funnier and more embarrassing childhood stories. After dinner, they had *café*, which Lindy said was like cappuccino, on the lanai and talked. He left Lindy out to star gaze and called his dad back into the kitchen, sharing with him that he wanted to mate Lindy according to the old ways.

His dad rubbed his stubble with two fingers. "It's not been done that way in decades, son. It would be good for the glen to see such a union. When would you like to do it?"

"We only have four more days here before we go back to spend a week in her realm. I'd like to have her as my wife before we go back to the Mortal Realm."

His dad's brows rose. "That's pretty quick. And your mother will have to come home early from her spa trip." With a thoughtful look, he called Laud and Juli into the kitchen, and they returned quickly. Clapping Crimson on the shoulder, he said, "My son is going to mate his bride according to the old ways during sunset in two days. Gather servants from the guild and make sure every available hand is working to make this the most memorable mating our glen has ever seen."

"Mom will like that," Crimson said as the two servants hurried away to begin preparations.

"Yes, she will like the spectacle of the thing, but it's not really about her or me. It's about you respecting your bride enough to vow yourself to her according to the old ways. With blood and iron and fire."

Nodding, Crimson felt the sting of tears but fought them back. Then he asked the question that had been on his mind since he had spoken to his commander. "Dad, will you be disappointed if I step down from the infantry?"

The shock on his dad's face told him that the question was completely unexpected. "Why on earth would I be disappointed?"

He fidgeted under his dad's concerned gaze. "Because I'm not going to live up to your name."

"Oh good night, Crimson! Are you serious? I never expected you to do everything that I did. Hell, if I could go back and do my life over, I would have stepped down from the infantry and spent more time at home." He pressed his hands into Crimson's shoulders and stared straight into his eyes. "I couldn't be more proud of you than I am right at this moment. You've had a wonderful career so far. Finding Lindy isn't the end of your life; it's just the beginning. I have no doubt that you'll continue to impress me and everyone else. Besides, you might find yourself living in the Mortal Realm with your sweet she-wolf, and then the military is definitely out of the picture. You're leading with your heart, Crimson. A father couldn't ask for more than that."

"Thanks, Dad." Crimson spoke the words on a whisper, afraid he was going to lose it and cry. He'd been worried that his dad would be disappointed in his choices, but he shouldn't have. His dad had always been his biggest supporter.

"The moment the healer put you in my arms when you were born, you became the son of my heart. My pride for you knows no bounds."

With a tight hug, his dad smiled at him and left him in the kitchen alone to gather his thoughts while he went out to visit with Lindy. Crimson joined them several moments later, enjoying how easily Lindy fit into his life. Eventually, she couldn't hide her yawns from him, and it was time to head home. Laud drove them, and Lindy fell asleep against Crimson's shoulder. After saying goodbye to Laud, he carried Lindy into his home—their home—and put her to bed.

He had a lot to do in the next two days, but the work was worth it because of Lindy. She was worth everything to him.

Chapter Fifteen

The following morning, Lindy and Crimson were enjoying breakfast when a woman's voice called from outside.

"Crimson Ta'rek! You invited me to your home to dress your bride, and you left on your protection spell. I'm insulted!"

"Oh, hades." Crimson jumped up from the chair as he spoke a few words and then raced to the front door.

He bowed at the waist, his hand sweeping out in front of him in a welcoming gesture. "Many apologies, Lafawnya. Please, do come in."

A short, round woman, with a pile of white-blonde curls on top of her head, harrumphed and stormed into the house. Two young girls who looked to be teenagers followed closely behind, carrying bolts of fabric and baskets of supplies.

Lafawnya glared up at Crimson with her hands on her hips. "You're just lucky that you're a distant cousin and I owe your father a debt after he stopped my parents from forcing me to mate a male I didn't love."

She turned her attention to Lindy and narrowed her eyes. "You. Go to the bedroom and strip. I'll be there in a moment." Jerking her hands at the two girls, she said, "Go with her and get things set up. I'll be joining you in five minutes."

The girls squeaked in alarm and moved to Lindy. "Quick, miss, we need to hurry! The madam doesn't like to be kept waiting."

Lindy looked at Crimson, who was smiling wryly. "Sorry, *chelle*. She's the best in the realm."

"Best what?" Lindy asked as the girls hurried her down the hallway.

"Dressmaker," one of the girls whispered.

Lindy led them into the room. The girls whipped around her like tiny brunette tornadoes, laying out the supplies they had carried in. One of them said, "Miss, please! She'll toss us out if you aren't undressed when she gets back here."

"Toss you out? Of the house?" She began to undo her top.

"No, we're apprentices. Madam is the best dressmaker in all the realm. Her family has been making gowns for the royal family and other high-born fae for generations. It's an honor to be chosen as an apprentice, but if she's displeased, she'll toss us out on our ears, and we'll never become dressmakers."

Lindy stripped and folded her clothes on the dresser. She was used to nudity because of the full moon shifts and had no problem being naked around others. Lafawnya stormed into the room and looked at Lindy, who was picking at her fingernails and watching the girls spread fabric out on the bed.

"You, girl. Stand here," Lafawnya said, pointing to a spot in front of her.

Lindy put her hand on her chest. "Me?"

"Anyone else naked and waiting for a dress? Yes, you. Don't dawdle, my time is very precious."

Lindy snorted to herself but moved to the spot. "My name is Lindy."

"What's your real name?" Lafawnya's eyes narrowed.

"Melinda."

Nodding, she grabbed Lindy's wrists and straightened her arms out to the side. One of the girls handed her a measuring tape. "That's a much prettier name."

Lafawnya spoke softly and the tape measure floated from her hand and moved through the air, lengthening along Lindy's arm. Lindy's eyes widened. "What the hell?"

One of the teens whispered, "It's a bespelled measuring tool. All of Madam's tools are magic."

Lafawnya called out measurements and one of the girls wrote them down in a small notebook. The tape measure floated back into her hand, and she closed her fingers around it. Leaning forward, she said, "Bend down so I can see your eyes."

She did as instructed, and the fae dressmaker peered into her eyes. She leaned back and Lindy straightened, and Lafawnya's eyes roved up and down Lindy's body for a long moment, and then she said, "Bring me the *talanic* fabric."

The teens both inhaled sharply, and Lindy looked over her shoulder at them. They seemed surprised.

Lafawnya said, "Your mate is going to vow himself to you in the *old ways*, Melinda. Did he explain it to you?"

"Not really."

"I'll leave it to him, then, but know that what he's going to do for you at sunset tomorrow is going to change things in this realm, in his life, and yours, forever."

That sounded ominous. "Is it dangerous?"

"Anything worth doing usually is in some way or another."

"I respect traditions, Lafawnya. My people honor our ancestors in many ways, including our mating and joining ceremonies. Crimson wants to do this because it's important to him, and that makes it important to me."

Lafawnya nodded, respect shining in her eyes. The teens brought Lafawnya a bolt of fabric that was pearl white. Lindy didn't think she had the skin tone to pull off a white dress, but she had a feeling if she opened her mouth that Lafawnya would use some kind of magic item to gag her. Crimson wouldn't have sent someone to help her if the woman didn't know what she was doing.

More words that Lindy didn't know were spoken, melodious and soft. The fabric lifted from her hands and began to unwind, draping itself around Lindy. When she saw what looked like two pairs of shears flying toward her, Lindy simply closed her eyes and tried very hard not to move.

For what felt like an eternity, all she could hear was the soft murmuring of the dressmaker and teens, the cutting sounds from the shears, and rustling fabric. She wondered what Lafawnya meant when she'd said that the ceremony would change the realm as well as their own lives. She knew she and Crimson were going to be married by fae standards the following night at sunset. She wished her mother and friends could join her, but the mating ceremony was strictly for the Fae Realm.

"Lovely," Lafawnya said.

Lindy opened her eyes and stared into a full-length mirror the teens were holding. She gasped in surprise. The dress was a gorgeous ball gown, a shade of blue that matched her eyes perfectly. The drape at the back of the dress made it appear as if she had wings folded against her back, and the pinched waist and low-cut bodice made her look like a pinup.

One of the teens handed Lindy a pair of satin sandals that matched the dress perfectly and were studded with what looked like diamonds. "The dress is beautiful, Lafawnya, thank you."

She bowed and then smiled. "It was my pleasure to dress the bride of our glen's only *wulfen*." She slipped a dark purple ring on Lindy's right index finger. "May you have a sweet life, Melinda, wolf from the Mortal Realm, and find much happiness with your mate."

Lindy thanked the dressmaker and the two teens after they helped her disrobe and hung the dress in the closet. She dressed in her regular clothes and walked them out to the front room, where Crimson said goodbye and held the door open for them.

"How was it, sweetheart?"

"She had scissors that came flying at me!"

He laughed. "Tools of the dressmakers' trade. She used to use brownies, but they don't live on this side of the mountain anymore."

"Brownies?"

"They're about the size of a gnome and have brown skin and hair. They are very helpful and like to make things."

"Why did they move to the other side of the mountain? What's on the other side?"

"The other side of the mountain is very dangerous. The Fae Realm is home not only to fae, but also to other creatures. Strange beasts, fae that have been rejected from our glens because of their criminal behavior, and other undesirable creatures. The closer you get to the top of the mountain, the colder it is. We weren't twenty feet up the face of the mountain, not even one-tenth of the way. The top of the mountain is covered in snow and ice and a layer of thick clouds. The side of the mountain facing our part of the realm is lush and green while the other side is void of anything but stone and dirt. There aren't glens in the traditional sense, but territories protected by the different groups."

"Why would the brownies live there if it's dangerous?"

"Some time ago, brownies decided they didn't want to work in servitude to fae any longer, so they moved to the other side of the mountain. They have magic that can make them and their homes invisible, so they live where they can do their own work and not have others telling them what to do."

"Well, I guess I won't ever meet a brownie, but they sound neat."

He cast the protection spell over the house and closed the door, turning with a low growl and snatching her against him. "You were gone quite a while, *chelle*. I missed you."

She sank against him, reveling in the feel of his lips when he kissed her and the way her body fit his so perfectly.

"Crimson Ta'rek!" A shrill voice screeched from outside their home while Lindy was reading a book about the mating ceremony and Crimson was working in the bedroom on his own outfit. "You slippery *wollbeast*!"

Lindy stood, setting the book on the low table in front of the couch.

Crimson came out of the bedroom. "Oh, hex."

"Who is that?" Lindy asked as the woman continued to screech Crimson's name and call him creatures that sounded very unpleasant.

"It's Giwyn."

"Ah. The one you found naked on the bed when you got out of the shower?" She smiled at him, and he snapped his teeth at her.

"I didn't ask for her to be there," he said indignantly.

"You sure you're really a wolf? I don't know any unmated males who would turn down pussy like that." She tapped her fingernail to her chin.

"You would have preferred that I ravaged her?" he snarled, and she laughed.

"Of course not, but it's kind of funny."

"It is not."

"Yeah, it is."

He grabbed her by the back of the neck and kissed her hard. "Is. Not."

Still snarling, he stormed through the front room and threw open the door. He appeared utterly calm when he leaned against the doorjamb and said, "You bellowed?"

Lindy moved to stand next to Crimson, and he took her hand and squeezed it. Giwyn was thin and willowy, with flame-red hair that looked anything but natural. She might have been pretty, if her face hadn't been screwed up into a haughty sneer.

"Your mother promised you to me, Crimson Ta'rek," she said angrily. "You kicked me out of your bed, and for what?" She looked at Lindy, and her lip curled up in disgust. "So you could rut like a beast with a commoner from the Mortal Realm? You know our ways, Crimson. She will never be accepted, no matter what ceremony you plan for yourselves, and you'll shame your family name and destroy your mother."

Crimson straightened from his casual stance and angled himself slightly in front of Lindy. "My mother will be fine, but I'll be sure to let her know you care. And as for my bride," his voice began to change from smooth and controlled to rough and deep, "there is nothing *common* about her or our mating. She's already been accepted by those who matter to me, and since you *don't*, I suggest you take the short road to Hades and get off my property."

Lifting one hand, he snapped his fingers and flames burst from the ground in front of Giwyn; she shrieked and fell back as a wall of fire built up between her and the house. She screamed in fright as Crimson lifted his hand and the flames grew higher and brighter. Lindy shielded her eyes from the intensity as Giwyn ran down the path and climbed hurriedly into a white carriage led by an orange horse that dashed away down the street as Crimson let the flames die.

Fanning herself to cool down, Lindy said, "Is she right?"

Crimson snorted. "She's never been right about anything to do with me."

"But your parents? Will our mating cause problems for them?"

"Of course not." He turned and pulled her inside the front room, shutting the door. He sat on the couch and pulled her onto his lap. Cradling her face in his hands, he kissed her sweetly and thoroughly and then said, "The only people who would find fault with our mating are those who don't believe in truemate spells or feel as if mating with those outside our realm is taboo. Those kinds of closed-minded people don't matter to me in the least, or to my father or my friends." He leaned back against the couch and hugged her close. "I don't know what my mother will think. She's probably home now, and I'm rather surprised she hasn't shown up to demand an explanation. One day, *chelle*, she'll realize that I'm happy with you, and she'll want to share in our joy. But if that day never comes, then that's okay, too. Because I wouldn't want my mother's approval if it meant I couldn't have you."

She leaned back far enough to look into his beautiful green eyes. Her heart swelled, and she opened her mouth to tell him that she loved him but decided it was too soon. She would tell him on the night of their mating, when they vowed themselves to each other in the *old ways*.

"Thank you for standing up for me. For us."

"It's what mates do."

The following morning, Crimson was out of bed and dressed by the time Lindy woke. He brought breakfast to her in bed and said, "I have to go help my father with some preparations for the ceremony tonight. I'll be back before dinner and will bring my parents' servants to help you get ready. My father will come to pick you up and take you to the ceremony."

He kissed her goodbye, and she lazed around in bed for a while before she got up and took care of the dishes. She had the whole day to herself, but nothing to do. She'd read the book on the *old ways* ceremony several times the day before and had read a volume of history of the Fae Realm as well. Although she had always thought fairies were creatures of peace and harmony, there was as much strife and war in their past as in the Mortal Realm. Wars between glens. Royal families fighting for control. Problems in the court system with bribery and discrimination. The fae version of racism based on powers was still clearly evident today, where those with noble powers were considered better than those with non-noble powers.

And then there was Hades Ridge, the mountain range separating the fae glens and what Crimson had said about those not welcome in the glens. According to the history of the realm, there had been wars fought from one side of the mountain to the other, but not in a long time. The military kept the mountain guarded, and those on the other side were content to keep to their own side.

Deciding she didn't want to read anymore, she headed to the bathroom and took a long, relaxing bath. She wanted to do something special with her hair but didn't have her curling iron or hot rollers, and of course, without electricity, there was no place for her to plug things in anyway. Finding a pair of shears in the kitchen drawer, she cut strips of fabric from a cotton tank she had brought with her. Then she separated her hair into sections, twisted them tightly, and coiled them into loops, using the strips of fabric to tie them in place. She was glad that Crimson wasn't home to see her looking so ridiculous.

She wished she had something constructive to do. If she were home, she would have cleaned, invited Faith and McKenna over to chat, or gone for a walk. Crimson's house was spic and span, and aside from making the bed, there was nothing for her to do. Faith and McKenna couldn't come visit because Crimson had to use his fairy ring to go into the Mortal Realm and would have to bring them here, and although he'd promised that if they chose to stay in the Fae Realm permanently she could go to visit her family and friends whenever she wished, she knew life would go on without her in Allen. She and her friends had always planned to raise their kids together.

She wasn't sure she wanted to stay in the Fae Realm. She was crazy about Crimson, and she thought his glen was neat, but she couldn't picture herself being the only real werewolf around. Missing the camaraderie of the pack on the full moon. Hunting in the woods where she'd grown up.

She reached up and touched her hair and knew it was now dry. Banishing the depressing thoughts to the far corner of her mind, she returned to the bathroom and undid the twisted loops of her hair. She and Crimson had three more days in his realm before they returned to the Mortal Realm for a week. She was looking forward to sharing her realm with him. And maybe he'd want to live there permanently. She smiled at her reflection as she ran a wooden comb through each lock of hair, mentally crossing her fingers that he would want to live in her realm.

When she was done with her hair, a mass of glossy, curly blonde locks adorned her head. She still had some time before his father came to get her.

Today is my wedding day, she thought giddily. Never in her wildest dreams had she ever thought she'd be marrying someone as amazing as Crimson. When she was little, she'd pictured her wedding like some gauzy, princess affair patterned after a fairy tale. As she'd gotten older, the fairy tale had morphed into a reality that hadn't been nearly as sweet. She'd imagined she would marry a human or wolf and the most exciting thing in her life would be the full moon hunts. Everything about her life since she'd met Crimson had been exciting, but more than the excitement that surrounded them was the love and affection she felt for him and that he felt for her. He hadn't told her that he loved her, but she could feel he did and knew he would tell her when the time was right for him. For her, it would be tonight. She would marry him in the traditions of his people and then she would give him her heart completely.

"Miss! Miss!" a voice called from outside of the house. Lindy's sensitive hearing picked it up, and she moved toward the front door as the female voice continued to call for her. "Miss! Please! It's Crimson, he's injured!"

Crimson was injured? Her pulse raced, and fear coursed through her. For a heartbeat, Lindy wondered if she should not open the door, but then she remembered the protection spell and knew no one could get in, even if she opened the door. As long as she stayed inside the house, she was safe from harm. Her heart began to pound as she opened the front door, worry for her mate making her wolf howl.

One of the young girls that had come with Lafawnya was standing just outside the protection spell. "Miss! Please come out. I'll take you to Crimson."

Lindy's hand gripped the door as she stood in the doorway. Something was off about the girl. She was trembling and rubbing her hands together, and her eyes were darting around nervously.

She'd never been told the names of the girls, so she said, "What's going on?"

The girl took in a trembling breath and whispered, "I'm sorry."

Something struck Lindy in the chest, and she gasped as paralysis spread quickly through her upper body. She tried to force her arm to slam the door, but she was frozen. A man stepped from behind a tree and walked quickly to the girl's side and grasped her arm. "Well done."

As tingling heat spread through Lindy and sleepiness overcame her, the girl said, "You said you'd help me if I helped you."

"And I will." With a quick motion, the man stabbed the girl in the neck, and she fell to the ground, clutching at the wound that spurted blood like a macabre fountain.

The man turned his gaze to Lindy, and he lifted his hand. She heard a tearing sound and watched as the protection spell was rent like a piece of fabric. The protection around the house sparked, the tear in the spell widening. Lindy desperately tried to move her body in any way, but the paralysis had taken over completely. All she could really do was breathe and blink her eyes. She couldn't even form words to speak.

The man spoke words she didn't know with a low but powerful voice, and a thin gold line extended from his fingertips, shooting through the air and wrapping around her neck. The golden line, which felt hot and tingled against her skin like electricity, wove down her body. He jerked his hand, and she felt her body being lifted from the ground. The sleepiness intensified as she neared him, and she wanted to bare her fangs at him and growl, free the wolf simmering under her skin, but she could do nothing but glare at him.

He was tall and thin, with long, black hair and a thin goatee. His eyes were a blue so pale that they were almost white, and she felt chilled to the core as she stared into his eyes.

"Why'd you kill Jilla?" Giwyn asked as she strode from the trees surrounding Crimson's home. Somehow, Lindy wasn't surprised to see the haughty fairy was involved in whatever was happening to her.

Lindy's eyes kept fluttering shut, but she forced them open, trying to take in all she could. In her mind, she screamed for Crimson, wondering if their connection as truemates was strong enough for him to know she was in trouble. If she died today, she would regret never telling him that she loved him.

"Because she was a liability," the man sneered.

Giwyn looked at Lindy with disdain. "Have a nice life, mortal. For however long it will last."

"Depends on who buys her," the man snorted.

Lindy tried to force her eyes to remain open, but they slid shut and refused to heed her demands. Her wolf howled for its mate as she felt her body being moved and heard the sound of hooves pounding furiously on the road.

And then...nothing.

Chapter Sixteen

Crimson hadn't liked leaving Lindy during the day of their mating, but there was still much to be done. He knew she would have gladly come along to help, but since he was doing things according to the *old ways*, it was the male's responsibility to ensure the ceremony went off without a hitch.

When his father had mated his mother, the females in his mother's family had handled everything, which was the modern way. The females decided on everything from the location of the vows to the food that would be served afterward. His father said he'd never been bossed around so much in his life as he had been the day he mated Crimson's mother. Generations ago, the females had begun to take over the planning and execution of the mating ceremonies, and they became less about the actual mating and more about the lavishness of the party.

But this was not a typical mating ceremony. With his father's help, he had scoured ancient texts to ensure the ceremony adhered to the *old ways* and respected his ancestors as well as Lindy. When he mated her tonight, those in attendance would know how much he valued mating her. He hadn't chosen her because his mother thought she was a good match socially. The truemate spell had brought them together, but her big heart, beautiful smile, and sweet nature were what made him want to mate her and vow himself to her forever.

The ceremony was going to be held in the garden behind his parents' home on a large marble stage. Riyad had been tasked with decorating the stage with beautiful and fragrant flowers.

Riyad came into the room where Crimson was polishing silver candlesticks that had been used by his great-great-great grandfather during his mating ceremony. They were heavy and ornate, and in desperate need of a good polish.

"I've finished the flowers."

Crimson looked up from the candlestick. "Thanks. For everything. I mean it."

Riyad leaned against the wall and folded his arms. "The *old ways* are complicated, but I have to admit that they're *resh*. When the glen sees what used to happen during mating ceremonies, there's going to be a demand for traditional matings."

"If the females will give up control of the ceremonies." Crimson chuckled, rubbing at a spot of tarnish. After inspecting the candlestick, he picked up another one and began to polish it.

"It seems as if females have no say any longer, anyway." Crimson's mother's voice rang out, her words sharp and laced with bitterness.

Crimson dropped the candlestick in surprise as his mother walked into the room. His father had gone the night before to the spa and told her about Lindy. She had returned with him, but when Crimson had shown up that morning, she had refused to see him. He wondered if she would refuse to attend the ceremony.

He picked up the candlestick and set it on the low table. "Mother, I would have talked to you earlier, but you refused to see me."

She hummed in her throat and looked at Riyad. He straightened suddenly and said, "Oh, sorry. I'll go back and check on the flowers."

When they were alone, his mother sat down on a high-backed chair and took several minutes to carefully arrange her skirt and settle into the chair. When she finally met his eyes, he could see the disappointment in the green depths.

Anger rose up inside him. Lindy was worried that she wouldn't be accepted by his mother, and here she was already disapproving of his mate. And he would absolutely not tolerate that. She opened her mouth to speak, but he jumped to his feet and spoke first.

"I spelled for Lindy, Mom. I knew you wouldn't stop sending females to my house until I found a mate. You forced my hand."

Her eyes narrowed. "So your mating is my fault?"

He threw up his hands. "Of course not! Lindy's the best thing that ever happened to me. Yes, I spelled for her because you were not listening to me about what I wanted, but I wouldn't change anything that happened because of it. I got the most wonderful woman in the world as my mate. Mom," he sat down on the table in front of her, "she accepts everything about me without question. She makes me want to be a better man. She's perfect for me, and I don't care if you're unhappy that she's from the Mortal Realm or that Dad and I planned the mating ceremony in the tradition of our ancestors. Tonight when the sun sets, I'm going to vow myself to Lindy forever. And then I'm going to spend the rest of my life making sure she's the most loved female who has ever lived."

He inhaled slowly, trying to calm down. He knew his mother couldn't take Lindy away from him, but his wolf was ready for a fight if she tried.

She cocked her head. "Are you quite done, Crimson?"

He frowned. "I...guess."

She cleared her throat delicately and then said, "I'm proud of you, son."

His mouth fell open. "You are?"

She nodded. "Yes. When your father first told me what you had done, I was furious." She paused for a moment and then continued. "Then he told me what my constant attempts to find you a mate were doing to you and how bitter and angry you'd become. I never meant for that to happen. I just wanted you to be happy."

"I *am* happy."

She smiled. "I can see that. And you're very protective of your Lindy."

Reaching forward, she grabbed both of his hands. "I misjudged you. Or, rather, I didn't listen. I thought if I sent enough eligible females to you that one of them would be your mate, but I was clearly wrong. Your father told me to stop, that I would push you away, but

I thought I knew best. I can admit when I'm wrong, Crimson, and I was wrong. I'm sorry for the grief I've caused you, and I hope you'll forgive me."

He hugged her. "Of course I forgive you, Mom."

She sniffled and leaned back, brushing tears from her cheeks with her fingertips. "Since your father refuses to allow me to make any changes to the itinerary tonight, I'd like you to take me to your home so I can meet your mate and help her get ready."

"Really?" A great weight lifted from his shoulders at her acceptance.

"Of course. I'm about to get a daughter, and maybe I can talk her into giving me some grandbabies soon."

Crimson chuckled. He would like that, too.

He stopped to tell his father and Riyad that he and his mother were heading home for a little while. After promising to return to finish helping, he assisted his mother into the carriage and sat next to her. Laud snapped the reins, and the horse began to trot.

"I asked your father if you were going to stay here or live in Lindy's realm, and he said he didn't know."

"I don't know yet either. I'm going to stay there for a week with her, and then we'll decide. Aside from the maw-serpent in the bed and missing her modern technology, I'd say she's enjoying herself."

"A maw-serpent?" his mother gasped.

He began to tell her about finding the serpent and his suspicion that Giwyn was responsible when he felt a stab of fear straight in his heart. He pressed his palm over his heart, and his wolf snarled. He swore he could hear his name being screamed.

Lindy!

He barked at Laud to move faster, knowing the horse could close the distance to the house faster than he could fly. He told his mother what he felt and her eyes widened in worry. He felt Lindy's fear as if it were his own. She was terrified and calling to him for help through their connection.

"Faster, damn it!" he shouted.

The fear he felt grew thicker until he was almost choking on it, and then just as suddenly as it had come, the fear cut off, and he was left feeling entirely bereft. He didn't know what it meant. He didn't want to think what it *could* mean.

He shouted for her in his mind, his wolf howling in distress. His house came into view, and he ripped off his shirt, letting his wings spring free from his back. Before the carriage stopped, he manifested his sword and leapt onto the walkway, racing forward. He could feel that the protection spell had been destroyed, and the stench of *wizard* clung to the air.

Hoping that she was in the house, he raced through each room, shouting her name, but finding no trace of her. He and Laud searched outside while his mother portal-called his father for help.

"Your father is on the way with reinforcements." His mother said as she came outside.

"I can smell her to this point," he gestured to the walkway, "and then she just disappears."

He'd never met a wizard who was good. Most of them dabbled in dangerous, black magic, carousing with demons and castaways on the other side of Hades Ridge. "I know where I have to go," he said, releasing his sword.

"Do you know who took her?" his mother asked, wringing her hands with worry.

"No." He shook his head and walked into the house and to the bedroom, where he removed a satchel from the closet. Although his sword was his favorite weapon, he had many other weapons in his home, and he filled the satchel with them.

He walked out of the bedroom and said, "Mom, I smelled Giwyn and one of the young assistants that Lafawnya brought with her. I smelled the young female's blood, and I think she was killed."

"Giwyn was involved?" Her hands clenched into fists. "I'll string her up by her bony fingers."

"I'm sure she'll deny everything, but I know what I smelled. Giwyn was here today, with the wizard and the girl. I'm certain she had something to do with Lindy's disappearance."

"I didn't think a wizard could be strong enough to break one of your protection spells. Yours are so powerful because of your *wulfen* nature."

"I didn't know that either."

It tore him to pieces. He had thought Lindy was safe in the house. He just hoped his carelessness would not lead to her death. He wouldn't be able to survive her death. He already knew that with absolute certainty. His wolf would go into the afterlife in search of her without delay, and Crimson would deserve to have his own life cut short.

"I never told her." He sat on the step and put his head in his hands. He could still smell her on his hands from when he'd held her that morning.

"Told her what?"

"That I love her. That I can't live without her."

His mother sat down and put her arm around him. "I'm sure she knows, Crimson. As soon as your father gets here, we'll find her and bring her home safely."

His home wasn't safe for her, though, and he realized that now.

Before long, his father, Riyad, and Merik were standing in front of Crimson's home, along with many of the males who Crimson had led into battle. Crimson explained the situation to them, and with a shout from Riyad, all the males extended their wings and roared a battle cry. They were with him. He'd never been so humbled.

After hugging his mother and thanking her for her support, he took to the sky with his father and the men he had served with and headed to the Ridge. On the other side of the mountain, his mate was waiting for him to rescue her, he was sure of it. And woe be to any male who touched even a hair on her head. Crimson would see him dead in a painful and horrible fashion.

Chapter Seventeen

Lindy woke up slowly. Her stomach rolled, and her head ached. Remembering that she was not safe inside Crimson's home, but had been drugged and taken, she forced her body to appear relaxed and took in a few, deep breaths. She listened intently with her eyes closed. She could tell that several people were around her because of the sound of their breathing. Drawing in several slow, deep breaths, she tried to decipher what she smelled. Aside from the ground under her, she could scent nothing else.

Her hands were tied in front of her with rough rope, but her legs were free. Opening her eyes, she saw that she was in a wooden cage in a clearing in the woods. She rolled to her butt and sat up, swooning for a moment as her head pounded and her vision blurred. Rubbing her thumb between her eyes, she groaned softly.

There were empty cages on either side of her. The clearing was surrounded by thick trees, but over the tops of them, she could see the mountains. They didn't look all that far. Maybe just a few miles. If she could shift, she could run and maybe find a cavern to hide in until whoever took her stopped hunting for her. Then she could climb the mountain and find Crimson. It would be difficult, but she had to get back to him.

The sound of heavy footsteps filled the air. Turning to the side, she saw four huge men with bulky forearms lumbering toward the cages. They wore loincloths made of dark fabric and no shoes. Long hair hung in matted clumps from their heads, and their squished faces reminded her of bulldogs. Fear inched up her spine as they came toward her, but she breathed through it and willed herself to be strong.

The huge men parted, and the man who had taken her came toward the cage with another man. She stifled the growl in her throat and glared at them.

"She is lovely, is she not, Nikao?" the man who had taken her remarked.

The other man was thin and tall, with wispy blond hair and blue eyes, a hawk-like nose and pursed lips. "I don't know, Crakin. She's awfully fleshy."

"Did you just call me fat?" she demanded.

Both men ignored her, and she closed her eyes, concentrating on her wolf. She could feel the drugs still in her system, but her wolf was there and ready, stronger than whatever potion she'd been given.

Clearing her mind, she opened her eyes and focused on the group of four huge creatures. Trolls, maybe. The enormous forearms made them look comical, and she bet from their stocky legs they couldn't run fast, either.

The rope rubbed against her wrists, chafing them. It was too tight for her to wiggle her hands free, but when she shifted, it wouldn't matter. The best plan was to wait until she was outside the cage and then shift.

Crakin gestured to the trolls. "Open the cage."

"What if she tries to run?" Nikao asked.

Crakin lifted a narrow vial from the pocket of his jacket. "She's not going anywhere."

Nikao shook his head. "If she's unconscious, no one will buy her."

"This is a lighter dose. It will make her sluggish and complacent."

One of the trolls lumbered forward. He flipped a latch on the top of the cage and threw open the lid. Reaching inside, he grabbed Lindy by the back of the shirt and hauled her out of the cage as if she were a sack of potatoes.

"Put me down!" She struggled, twisting her body to try to get free, but the troll didn't let go of her shirt.

Crakin dipped the tip of a dart into the vial, and Lindy knew she had to take the opportunity to flee or she might never see Crimson again.

Exhaling, she let herself go into her shift, pushing her body to change quickly. The men shouted in surprise as she slipped from her clothes and the rope fell away. She hit the ground on four paws and ran for the mountains, not daring to look back.

The forest raced by her as she kept her eyes trained on the mountains rising up in the distance. She didn't know if she was being followed, and she wasn't about to stop and check. Her feet ached, and her body was sore as she pushed herself to get to the mountains.

The ground changed from mossy to rocky as she cleared the trees. She paused for only a heartbeat, finding a narrow trail that led up the mountain and headed for it. The sun set while she ran, but she could see enough to pick her way up the mountain. She searched as she climbed, hoping to find a cavern like Crimson had taken her to.

She stopped on the trail and sat down on her haunches. She was exhausted. She'd never pushed her body so hard in her shift. All she wanted was a cold drink of water and a long nap. Her head dropped, and she let out a soft whine. She wished that Crimson was there with her.

Shaking herself out of her exhaustion, she pushed on, knowing that stopping on the trail was a bad idea. She could rest when the sun came out.

Her paw stepped on dry branches that cracked, and she paused. She sniffed and scented bread. Was she going crazy? The scent of bread came from the right, and she turned her nose in that direction and smelled the rock. But it wasn't rock, it was soft like a sponge. Pushing gingerly on the spongy material, she caught the scent of bread again and growled lightly. She took a step closer, and her paws suddenly went out from under her. The spongy material split apart, and she tumbled down a smooth, stone ramp, her body bouncing and jarring, knocking into every jutting rock.

Her head cracked hard against a stone, and she felt herself roll to a stop as she slipped into unconsciousness, unsure of where she was or whether she would ever see her mate again.

Cold water dribbled into Lindy's mouth, waking her. She swallowed and choked, coughing slightly. Sitting up, she banged her head on a rock and winced, groaning.

"Ouch, damn it."

Something small and warm touched her knee as she opened her eyes and looked down. The small, warm thing touching her was a small creature. It had tan skin and wispy brown hair. Its eyes were golden-brown.

"Shush now," the creature said with a lilting, feminine voice. "There is nothing to harm you here in our home."

Lindy looked around and found herself surrounded by dozens of the little creatures. The tallest among them were no more than two feet tall, each with the same tan skin and wispy brown hair.

Licking her lips again, she looked around for an exit but found nothing except rock walls. She must have fallen inside the mountain. The ceiling of the cave was just above her head and not tall enough for her to stand. Small homes made of wood were scattered around the cave and what looked like a hot spring was in one corner.

"What are you?" Lindy asked.

The one who had given her water smiled at her. "We're brownies. My name is Veril."

"It's nice to meet you, Veril. My mate told me that some of you used to work in the fae glens for the fairies."

There was a murmur of discontent, and Veril said, "We did, but we found that the fairies were happier taking credit for our work than thanking us for what we did. We love to work, but we also love to be appreciated."

Lindy remembered suddenly that she was in her human form, which meant she was naked. Looking down, she discovered she was wearing a simple but elegant shift. It was the color of pine needles and knit of soft, thick yarn.

"Thank you for dressing me while I was unconscious. It's lovely."

Veril preened. "It was our pleasure. It's not every day that a mortal-realm werewolf tumbles into our hidden home."

"I smelled bread."

Veril chuckled, and the others did as well. "It was our baking day."

As if on cue, food was brought to Lindy, and as she ate, she told the brownies about her kidnapping.

The leader of the brownies, a stocky male named Levrin, shook his head. "That Crakin is a menace. The she-fae who hired him to take you was foolish. If he planned to sell you at the *merash*, then he will find her and sell *her* instead."

"What is a *merash*?" Lindy asked, sopping up meat gravy with a thick slice of bread.

Levrin's wife, Hior, shuddered. "You might call it a slave auction in your realm. Dark wizards like Crakin make money by kidnapping and selling supernatural creatures from this realm and others. You're very lovely, and Nikao is a sex slave trader, so the *merash* was most likely for those looking for sex slaves. I'm afraid your future would have been a very bad one indeed if you had not escaped."

"I don't think they knew I could shift," she said. "They seemed very surprised."

"It's possible he believed you to be human. Regardless, we're happy to offer you protection."

"I'd like to get to my mate. Can you show me how to make it to the other side of the mountain so I can get to him?"

"Better than that," Levrin said. "We can take you to his home."

She grinned, and tears filled her eyes. "You can?"

"Of course. We're not fairies, but we do have magic," Yunni, Veril's daughter said.

Levrin nodded. "It will be our pleasure."

Lindy wiped at the tears that fell to her cheeks. "Thank you so much. For saving me and protecting me."

Levrin bowed, and the other brownies ducked their heads. "We were happy to do it."

While the brownies prepared the portal that would take her to Crimson's home, she washed her hands and face in the pool of the hot spring. She crawled on her hands and knees to avoid hitting her head on the ceiling, and knelt next to Veril and Yunni.

Levrin arranged some brightly colored rocks into a circle and spoke a few words. The brownies surrounded her, and Levrin said, "I would send you with my best fighters to ensure you are safe until you reach your mate."

A handful of male brownies wearing black trousers with swords strapped to their backs came to stand near her. One of them stepped forward and went down on one knee. "We would see you safe, she-wolf, until you are back in your mate's arms."

She smiled in gratitude. "Thank you."

Veril said, "Yunni and I will come as well."

Lindy said, "I appreciate the company."

Levrin asked for Lindy to extend her hand toward him. When she did, he positioned her hand over the center of the stone circle and took a small dagger, the size of a letter opener, and made several quick strikes across her flesh. She winced, but the pain passed quickly. He turned her hand over, and a few drops of blood fell onto the stones.

He said, "The blood of your mate is within your own blood, she-wolf Lindy. The portal will take you to his home. My people and I wish you a safe journey and a swift reunion with the one that you love."

"Thank you all for everything," she said. The six warriors and the two females put their hands on Lindy as Levrin began to chant. A bright glow rose from the circle, multi-hued like a rainbow and sparkling like the sunlight on water. It grew until it enveloped her with warmth, as if she were standing outside on a hot summer day.

Closing her eyes as the glow became too bright, she felt her body move and the air around her rush, and then she felt thick grass underneath her knees.

Opening her eyes, she found herself staring at Crimson's house and a very surprised woman.

She'd come home.

But where was Crimson?

Chapter Eighteen

Crimson smashed his fist into the face of the dark wizard named Crakin.

"Tell me where my mate is!" Crimson roared. He was struggling to keep his wolf under wraps. His beast wanted to tear Crakin apart with his claws.

Crimson and his friends had been searching for Lindy for almost an entire day. The horse and carriage tracks leading from his home ended abruptly at the bottom of the mountain. The horse lay dead, and the carriage had been set on fire. He could sense dark magic had been used, and it only confirmed his belief that she had been taken by a wizard. As far as he knew, wizards only kidnapped for two reasons: for sacrifice or sale. Although he didn't want to think about Lindy being sold in a *maresh,* he preferred that thought to her being slaughtered for some dark ritual.

They didn't know where the wizard had gone, so they were unable to open a portal. He had tried a location spell for Lindy, but it had been unable to tell him where she was. He felt as if she was still alive, and he assumed the reason he couldn't spell for her location was because she was being shielded by dark magic. They'd had to fly over the mountain, which had cost them precious time. Then they split up, and he, his father, and Riyad went one direction while Merik and the others went in another.

It had taken hours before he'd finally caught a faint scent of her. He followed it to a clearing just outside of Balladat City, which was known for its *mareshes.* There, he'd found the cage where Lindy had been kept.

It hadn't taken long to find the male who had taken her. There were three distinct scents near the cage: the wizard who stank of sulfur and ash, a fae male, and trolls. He wasn't worried about the trolls. They were stupid creatures that only followed the orders of those who ruled over them. He'd bet that they belonged to the fae male or the wizard.

First, they found the fae male named Nikao, who readily gave up the wizard, Crakin. Nikao had been restrained and was going to be taken back to the other side of the mountain to stand trial for his crimes. Crimson had a feeling that besides attempting to buy Lindy, he had done many, horrible things to others as well, and his crimes would need to be documented. From Nikao's information, they'd found Crakin easily, but finding out what had happened to Lindy was proving difficult.

Crakin spit blood on the ground and laughed. "Your she-bitch is gone. Hit me all you like, you will never see her again."

Riyad had restrained the wizard with thick vines filled with thorns, which were keeping the wizard kneeling on the ground. Crimson snarled and let go of the tight hold on his wolf a little. He felt his eyes change color, his fangs dropped from his gums, and his claws pushed out from his fingertips. Growling darkly, he gripped Crakin's neck with his hands and dug his claws into his flesh.

He snarled and said, "I will not kill you quickly. I will kill you slowly and painfully."

There was just a glimmer of fear in Crakin's eyes. Crimson tightened his hold and reached his other clawed hand to grasp Crakin's arm. He drew his hand up and opened his mouth widely over Crakin's wrist. Crimson hid his disgust at the stench of the male's skin that made him want to retch. He would do anything to see Lindy back in his arms. Anything.

With a swift motion, he snapped his jaws around Crakin's wrist, and the bones cracked. Crakin tried to scream, but he could do no more than gurgle because Crimson held his throat in one hand.

"Tell me," Crimson said.

Crakin panted, his eyes wide with fear, but he remained quiet. Crimson opened his mouth again, moving up to the elbow joint of Crakin's arm. Just before Crimson would have bitten down again, Crakin whispered, "Wait! Please! Wait! I'll tell you!"

Crimson released his hold on the wizard, and Crimson's father and Riyad grabbed him by the shoulders to keep him from falling over. Crakin cradled his broken wrist against his chest.

"The she-wolf fled into the mountains. She was too fast for the trolls to grab her, and when I cast a tracking spell for her, I lost track of her on the mountain. It's like she vanished."

Crimson clenched his hands into fists. "You lie! Tell me where she is!"

Crakin tried to scoot backward but couldn't move because of the thorny vines. "I'm not, I swear!"

Riyad gave him a shake. "What were you going to do with her?"

"Nikao was going to sell her as a sex slave in the *maresh*. I was told she was human, or I would have used a different potion to keep her from getting away."

Crimson moved closer. "Who told you that she was human?"

Crakin grinned suddenly, and his lips moved as he whispered very softly, his eyes flashing. Crimson manifested his sword and thrust it through Crakin's thigh and into the ground, skewering him into the dirt. Crakin screamed in pain, the transportation spell he was casting stopped in its tracks.

"Try to spell yourself out of that, asshole. Tell me where my mate is!"

Crakin seemed unable to do anything except cry and try to pry the sword from his leg with his good hand.

Riyad looked at Crimson, frowning. "You should try a location spell for her."

"I already did."

"That was before. It's been hours. If she escaped, then you might be able to find her now."

Crimson moved away from the group and gathered several stones, arranging them in a circle in front of a thick tree. He used his fangs to pierce his palm and let his blood drop onto the stones as he cast the spell to locate Lindy. Location spells were normally done with candles and an item belonging to the one that was supposed to be found. Crimson's blood was mixed with Lindy's because they had shared blood when they mated. She was a part of him forever. The important part of the candle was the flame, and he called his power forth and lit the drops of blood on fire, laying his hands on the tree and willing his power to find Lindy.

An image appeared, hazy like he was looking through frosted glass. He saw Lindy sitting on a hide couch surrounded by brownies and his mother sitting nearby with a cup of tea.

Hades! She was at his home!

Scattering the stones with his hand to break up the circle, he said, "She's home! Lindy made it home!"

Riyad and Crimson's father smiled in relief. His father said, "Riyad and I will wait for the authorities and contact Merik and the others. We'll find out how this *wolly-mouthed tryuo* found Lindy and was able to capture her. Go home to your mate."

Crimson embraced his dad and his best friend. "Thank you."

"You can thank me by naming your firstborn after me," Riyad called as Crimson took to the sky.

Crimson laughed, happiness blurring his vision as tears filled his eyes. His mate was home and safe. He flew as fast as he could towards home.

Chapter Nineteen

Lindy sipped at the *selli-root* tea Crimson's mom had made for her as she sat on the couch. Three of the warrior brownies were sitting on the floor in front of the couch, their swords drawn while the other three were outside patrolling. Crimson's mom, Thalia, told her the protection spell had been destroyed by a powerful wizard, and that Crimson could cast it again when he came home.

Lindy was worried about him. She'd been back at his home for two hours. Thalia had tried to contact him, but had been unable.

Veril and Yunni were sitting on the couch between Lindy and Thalia, nibbling on crackers. Veril said, "Your mate will figure out where you went soon enough, Lindy. He'll come storming through the door any moment, I'm sure."

"I must say," Thalia said, "the dress you made for Lindy is lovely. The weaving is so delicate."

Lindy also liked the dress and had complimented the brownies several times. Veril blushed, her tan skin pinking. "Thank you, Thalia."

While they were waiting for Crimson to come back, Veril told Lindy about the hidden entrance to their cavern. The cavern was hidden by a type of Fae magic, and Veril believed Lindy was able to not only find the cavern but fall into it because she was not in any way Fae or from the Fae Realm.

Lindy's wolf sat up, and she stood. "He's coming."

"How can you tell?" Thalia asked in surprise.

"I can feel him," Lindy answered.

She had taken two steps toward the front door when it was thrown open, the knob cracking against the stone wall. Crimson stood in the doorway looking like a pissed-off angel, with his white wings spread wide and his eyes glowing bright red.

Lindy's mouth fell open as he stalked to her. Her voice was caught in her throat as emotion welled up inside her. With little more than a grunt of acknowledgement, Crimson hauled her over his shoulder, and she found herself upside down between his wings as he stomped back to the bedroom and slammed the door closed.

He righted her quickly, and her head swam. Her back pressed to the wall as he caged her in, his palms flattened on either side of her. "I love you."

Her mouth fell open in surprise. "You do?"

He growled. "Yes. I swore to myself that the first thing I would say to you was how I feel about you. I love you."

The red faded from his eyes until she was staring into the pure, beautiful green eyes of the man she loved. She cupped his face. "I love you, too, Crimson. I thought I wouldn't get to tell you."

He kissed her, and then he pulled back abruptly. His hands roamed down her arms. "Are you hurt? What happened? Tell me everything."

He picked her up, more gently this time and with less growling, and set her on the bed. While she told him what had happened, he paced in front of her, occasionally asking for more details or snarling.

He nodded when she finished the story. "We found the fae and the wizard, and they are both being held for trial. My father and friends are handling things. But that leaves Giwyn."

She reached for his hand. "I'm sorry."

He looked surprised. "What for?"

"I shouldn't have opened the front door. He wouldn't have been able to get to me if I had left it shut."

He went to his knees in front of her and took both of her hands in his. "It wouldn't have mattered. He was very powerful. The spell he used was more powerful than my protection spell, and he would have gotten inside no matter what. I'm the one who's sorry."

"Why?"

"Because I should not have trusted that you were safe. I was foolish, and I almost lost you. I won't take that chance again."

"You can't stay glued to my side forever, Crimson."

"Yes, I can." He stood and pushed her backward, leaning over her.

She laughed. "What about when I have to pee?"

"Be serious, *chelle*," he groused.

"I am! I don't pee with an audience." She placed her palms on his chest and felt the heat of his skin. "I love you, Crimson."

"Fine. You can pee alone, but other than that, forget it." With a soft growl, he kissed her and whispered against her lips, "I love you. I love you so much."

Out in the front room, Crimson spoke to the warrior brownies and thanked them for their help. Crimson invited all the brownies to stay for the mating ceremony, and they seemed very pleased to be able to do so.

Crimson used the portal to contact his commander and explained what Giwyn had done. Fenick was incensed that the female had been part of something so terrible and promised to find her swiftly and see her to trial.

Lindy said, "Was your commander pissed because he likes you so much?"

He shook his head. "It's a serious crime to try to destroy a mating. Her punishment would be more severe if you had been physically injured or killed, but it is still a grievous offense. She will not see daylight for many years, and her family will be shamed."

"Good."

Thalia chuckled. "Are you two up for the ceremony still? We can have it tomorrow evening. That will allow time for everyone to get home safely and rest."

Crimson nodded, looking stern. "I want to be mated officially as soon as possible."

Lindy agreed wholeheartedly.

Thalia stayed until Desmin, Merik, Riyad, and the other males returned to Crimson's home. Lindy hadn't met his best friends officially, having been hustled away from them her first night in the realm when they'd been busted at the hot springs.

"We're glad you were able to escape," Riyad said, smiling at Lindy. Riyad leaned in to give her a hug, and Crimson snarled so loudly that it made everyone but Lindy take a step back. She wasn't surprised or worried by the noise he made. He was a wolf and they were possessive creatures with their mates.

"Thank you for helping Crimson. I feel better with those assholes behind bars." It still amazed her that Giwyn thought nothing of Lindy being sold as a sex slave. Lindy had hated some females before in her life, but she never would have wished sexual servitude on any of them. Giwyn gave new meaning to the term "vindictive bitch."

"…it means that we'll live in her realm," Crimson said, and Lindy brought her attention back to him.

"What?"

Crimson snuggled her a bit closer to his side, which was a nearly impossible feat since she was plastered against him. "I said that it's too dangerous here for you, and I think the best thing to do is live in your realm."

She was both happy and worried. "Are you sure? The people who took me are in prison. The danger from them is gone."

He leaned down, kissed her cheek, and whispered, "Later."

She hummed in her throat and nodded, saying nothing.

After thanking his family and friends once more, she and Crimson helped the brownies settle in for the night on the couch, with the warriors insisting on standing guard around the house overnight. Lindy and Crimson went to bed.

After they made love, Crimson rolled onto his back and pulled her with him. His fingertips twirled across her shoulders as he stared at the ceiling for several moments in silence.

"The loneliest times for me are on the full moon. When I was a teenager, Riyad and Merik would go out hunting with me, but it just aggravated my wolf because they weren't like us. I never told anyone that; I never shared much about my beast because, although people like my friends and my parents try to understand, they just can't. My mom said that she wished my biological father's family had been alive. He was an only child and his parents were much older when he was born and they died before he even met my mom. When I became a *wulfen*, she tried to locate his former pack, but they had disbanded and left the area, and since they weren't family anyway, she thought I was better off."

"You must feel torn in half sometimes, between the beast that wants things the fae part of you doesn't understand." She stroked her hand across his chest, loving the way his muscles flexed under her touch.

"I muzzled the wolf a lot." He looked at her with a smile. "He's very bossy."

"They can be." She planted her hands on either side of him and straightened her arms, looking down into his handsome face. "Crimson, we can be our own pack here. I don't want to take you from your family."

"You're my family now, Lindy. I know we could be happy here, but aside from the safety issue, I find myself longing to be part of a pack and run with other wolves. If you think they'll accept me."

A lightness settled over her. "They'll accept you because you're my mate. On the next full moon, the alphas can preside over our mating, and they'll welcome you into the pack."

He pulled her down and rolled her onto her back. "Tomorrow we're following my people's traditions, and then we'll leave for your realm. We can keep our home here and visit whenever we like."

He leaned down to kiss her, and she murmured, "Sounds like a good plan to me."

The following afternoon, she was back in the bedroom with Thalia, Veril, and Yunni, who were helping her get ready for the ceremony. Crimson was supposed to get dressed at his parents' home, but he had refused to leave her alone again. Crimson's commander had contacted them earlier in the day to explain that the military had been unable to find Giwyn, and it was believed she had disappeared so she wouldn't get into trouble for her part in the scheme. Crimson had gone berserk, nearly shifting into his wolf form with the news. She'd managed to get him calmed down by speaking to him softly and petting him like she'd seen some mated females in the pack do when their mates were wound up. Until Giwyn was found, Lindy didn't think Crimson would relax.

She was not necessarily relaxing herself. After all, that tricky she-fairy had almost gotten her sold into sexual slavery just because she was a sore loser. Crimson wouldn't feel that she was safe until Giwyn was in custody. Lindy was a live-and-let-live sort of gal, but Giwyn was a whack job and needed to be put away.

Lindy looked at herself in the full-length mirror. Her long hair was curled in ringlets that fell past her shoulders and reminded her of golden curling ribbon. The dress fit her beautifully. Her face practically glowed. Her eyes were bright, and her cheeks were pink. She wore no makeup save for some lip stain made from a dark pink fruit that Yunni gave her.

Thalia joined Lindy and looked at her in the mirror. "I made a lot of mistakes, Lindy. I'm sorry for my part in your kidnapping and for making you feel inadequate. My son is lucky to have you in his life, and I'm blessed to have you as a daughter."

Lindy didn't blame Thalia for Giwyn being crazy. She couldn't have known that she would become so obsessed with Crimson. But she knew Thalia carried guilt over what had happened.

"Forgiven and forgotten," Lindy promised, squeezing her hand.

There was a short knock on the door, and Thalia said, "That's your mate. He's an impatient thing, isn't he?"

Crimson said through the door, "I'm not impatient."

Lindy laughed as Thalia opened the door. The room fell silent as Crimson stared at her and she stared at him. He looked amazing. Black leather trousers stretched over his legs, and he wore black knee boots. His wings were out, like twin feathered shields behind his body, and he wore no shirt. Around his forearms were thick leather cuffs, decorated with symbols made of twisted gold wire. A sword hung from his side, the handle glinting with a ruby the size of a silver dollar.

He dropped to one knee and rested his fist over his heart, bowing his head. "You are so lovely, my mate. I am honored to pledge my life to you and to bind myself to you forever in the ancient ways of my people."

She closed the distance and stood before him. He raised his head slowly, his eyes flashing from green to red, the way they did when he was aroused. "I'm honored, Crimson. To have you as my truemate, my friend, my protector, and the only male I've ever given my heart to."

He stood and pulled her close, wrapping one arm around her waist and resting his fingertips along her jaw. "Mine."

She couldn't help but grin. "I wouldn't want to be anyone else's."

Veril clapped her hands. "It's so romantic."

Lindy laughed, and Crimson smiled. "It sure is," Lindy agreed.

So that her dress didn't get dirty, Crimson carried her from the house to the waiting carriage. He rode with her and his mom, and the brownies rode behind them in another carriage. Lindy leaned against his shoulder, and he cuddled her closer. "Just a few more hours and we'll be bonded forever, sweet love."

"And then what?" She peeked up at him through the veil of her lashes.

"Then I'm going to take you back to our home and spend the night reminding you why we're meant to be together."

As if she needed a reminder. No one had ever rocked her world the way Crimson did. Everything about him seemed made just for her.

The carriage stopped in front of his parents' home. The sun had set, but candles and lanterns lit the entire outside of the house and the walkway leading to the back where the ceremony was to take place. Thalia told her a traditional fae mating was very similar to a human marriage, with the couple vowing to each other in front of an official and their families, followed by a meal and party. But their *old ways* mating was going to be different because, although Lindy was going to be vowing herself verbally to Crimson, his vows to her were going to be done through deed and not word alone.

Their people had stopped using the *old ways* several generations ago as they modernized. Like most traditional things, some of the current marriage traditions were based on ancient ones, but the actual ceremony she and Crimson were going to go through was nothing like what the fae did now. Lafawnya said their mating would change the realm forever, and Lindy thought she meant that people would see the *old ways* and it would rekindle a desire to use them again.

Crimson came around the carriage and held his hands out. She leaned out of the carriage with her hands on his shoulders, and he lifted her easily and set her on the stone path.

"You look so beautiful, *chelle*," he said, twining one of her curls around his finger. "I'm the luckiest male in the realm."

Tears stung her eyes, and she blinked them away. "I love you, Crimson."

He pressed his lips to her forehead and inhaled. "I love you, sweet mate."

Taking her hand, he led her along the torch-lit path around the side of the house and into the backyard. She gasped in surprise to see so many people. Risers had been set up around a stage where the ceremony was going to take place. Hundreds of fae sat in gilded chairs on the risers. One entire riser was filled with men with feathered wings, and she knew they were soldiers in the military like Crimson.

They walked on the stone path between two risers, and the crowd went silent save for the many feminine gasps of appreciation for her gown and, she was sure, how handsome her mate was. As they drew nearer to the stage, lilting music from stringed instruments filled the air. It wasn't the traditional wedding march, but it was beautiful. Crimson stopped them at the bottom of four crystal stairs leading up to the stage that appeared to be made of gold marble. Around the stage, tall posts made of white marble were covered with lavender ribbon and tulle and draped with ivy vines and tiny twinkling lights. Above them, the dark sky was filled with stars as if the universe had come out to witness their mating.

A man that Lindy didn't know came to stand on the stage at the top of the stairs. He had long, white hair and a beard that reached the top of his trousers. He wore a velvet frock coat of dark red, adorned with garnets and rubies.

The music ebbed and then disappeared entirely. The man, who looked to be in his eighties, cleared his throat and said, "Enter ye onto this sacred stone to vow yourself to your truemate according to the *old ways*, Crimson Ta'rek?"

Crimson bowed at the waist. "I do, Elder Horus."

Elder Horus nodded once and moved away from the stairs, and Crimson took Lindy's elbow again and led her up the crystal stairs. She hadn't been able to see what the stage really looked like from the ground, but now that she was on top of it, she was amazed at what she saw. The solid slab of marble was several feet thick and bigger than her bedroom. In the center of the stone, a stand made of dark metal held a stone pot over a fire of blue flames. The bottom of the stone pot was red with heat, and smoke rose from the inside. Three metal poles several feet in length stuck out from inside the pot.

Elder Horus, who had blue wings veined with yellow, stood behind the pot with a large open book in his hands. To the right and left of the pot were Riyad and Merik. They were wearing their military jackets, their wings spread out behind their backs through special slits cut into the fabric.

There was a rustling sound behind them, and Lindy looked over her shoulder to see a line of people moving up the stairs and parting to walk down either side of the stage. Each person carried something in their hands, and when they stopped moving and faced toward the center of the stage, Lindy was able to see that they were all fae. Their wings were all different colors, which Crimson had explained meant that they had different powers.

Elder Horus looked at Crimson and Lindy, then cast his gaze around the perimeter of the stage. Then he said with a loud voice, "Be welcome ye delegates of the Fae Guilds. From far have ye traveled to witness the mating of these two." Turning his attention back to them, Elder Horus said, "Face your intended."

Crimson and Lindy turned to face each other, their hands clasped between them. Her heart pounded with excitement and joy as she stared into the beautiful face of her mate.

"The gifts of the Fae Guilds," Elder Horus said, "are presented now."

A fae with golden wings stepped from the side and stood in front of her and Crimson. In his hand was a strand of delicate, blue flowers on a vine of tiny, purple leaves. He wove the vine around their clasped hands. "The *blosomfae* bless your union and wish you a beautiful mating, as lovely as the flowers that bind you together."

He moved back to the line as another fae joined them, a female with blue wings. She gave them the gift of water in a stone container that she poured out at their feet, so they would never be thirsty. The next fae had pearly wings and gave them the gift of the air, a breeze captured in a glass jar that she set at their feet so they would always feel the wind at their backs. A male fae with orange wings brought them a leather satchel of dirt that they would always have a fertile field to provide for them.

Elder Horus said, "The final gift from the fae is Melinda's wedding band, forged in the hottest of fires as only a *firefae* can control." A female with blue and yellow wings strode forward and slipped a ring onto Lindy's left ring finger. It felt warm, and a tingle raced up her arm.

Elder Horus said, "Melinda Vincent, do you vow yourself to your mate, Crimson Ta'rek, the Fae Realm Wulfen, from this moment until time ends? Do you vow yourself to him alone?"

As Crimson had coached her, she answered with a voice that only slightly trembled, "I so vow."

Crimson smiled at her, and her vision blurred as tears filled her eyes.

"Crimson Ta'rek, do you vow yourself to your mate, Melinda Vincent, the Mortal Realm she-wolf, from this day until time ends? Do you vow that you will protect her and your offspring with your life? Do you vow that you will keep her in happiness for the rest of her days? Do you vow to love her, and her alone, as no other has ever loved?"

Crimson's eyes bled to the red of his beast for only a moment, and then he said, "I so vow."

Merik and Riyad came to stand in front of them. Riyad unwound the vine of flowers from their hands and carefully draped it over Lindy's shoulders. Crimson released her hands after a quick squeeze and took two steps away from her. She'd read the history of the *old ways* and knew in her mind what was going to happen, but to see it unfold before her was nerve-wracking. As Elder Horus began to read in an ancient language, Riyad and Merik pulled two of the poles out of the pot, and Lindy swallowed hard at seeing the glowing brands on each end.

She held Crimson's gaze as Riyad and Merik lifted the brands and brought them down on his biceps. The scent of burning flesh filled the air immediately, but he never flinched or uttered a sound as the brands sizzled. They pulled the brands away, and in their wake were the burned images of the brands, fae language script edged with flames. They were his vows to her, his promise that he would be everything to her because she was everything to him.

The brands clinked against the pot as they were put back in place, and then Elder Horus handed Crimson a dagger that looked like it had been chiseled from stone. He cut across his left palm, and the thick wound welled with blood that dripped into a chalice Elder Horus held underneath his hand.

"The blood of the warrior is his life, given freely today to honor his mate," Elder Horus said, lifting the chalice and speaking a few words in a low tone. The contents blazed and sparked, and the acrid scent of smoke swirled around them.

The third brand was pulled from the pot, glowing with heat, and the elder held it out over Crimson's open, bleeding hand.

"Vow yourself through flesh and blood and iron, young fae. Prove yourself worthy of your mate."

"I so vow." Crimson spoke with strong, sure words, reaching up to grab the brand and wrapping his hand around it. He let out a low growl as he looked at her, his fangs peeking from his parted lips and his eyes flashing from red to green. "I. So. Vow." He snarled the last word and lifted his head in a joyous howl, releasing the brand and holding his hand up toward the heavens.

The fae around them cheered. Crimson closed the distance to her and held out his hand, palm up. She gasped in surprise to see the scar on his palm read "Melinda." She hadn't realized that the third brand had been prepared with her name.

She lifted his hand and kissed the healing mark.

"Mine," he growled and pulled her close, bending her backward and kissing her hard. The crowd roared again, and she blushed, even though she loved kissing him.

He righted them both slowly, and her head swam as her heart pounded with joy. Nothing had ever felt as right as her life did at that moment. She'd been unhappy for a long time, but as Crimson had said, the paths they'd chosen over the course of their lives had led them to this place. And there was no place she'd rather be.

Chapter Twenty

What Crimson wanted to do was toss Lindy over his shoulder and race home to ravage her a few dozen times before sunrise. What he *had* to do, however, was stay right there on the stage with his beautiful mate and greet the dignitaries from the various guilds first.

Elder Horus led them to the dignitaries and introduced them, and then Crimson and Lindy shook their hands and accepted their blessings. When they had met them all, they were led to the edge of the platform to stand before the gathered fae. Elder Horus lifted his voice. "I present the newly mated Crimson and Melinda Ta'rek of the Fae Realm. What has been witnessed here tonight let no one tear apart."

Crimson's parents waited for them as he walked Lindy down the steps and past the cheering fae. His mom immediately hugged Lindy, and the two sniffled, trying not to cry.

"I'm so proud of you, son," his dad said, hugging him.

"Thanks, Dad," he said, fighting the urge to cry.

After hugging his mom, he followed them into the house where a private party was set up for their family and close friends. The rest of the guests would be entertained outside where Crimson and Lindy would make an appearance before they left for the evening. The party would go until dawn, but he had no intention of staying that long.

"You look like you have wicked things on your mind," Lindy whispered into his ear.

He just grinned.

The meal passed quickly, although it felt to him and his beast like an eternity. When it was done, he carried her back outside to the stage and they waved goodbye to the crowd that was well on the way to being six sheets to the wind. They said goodbye to his family and the brownies, who promised to come visit whenever they were in the realm, before he settled her into the carriage, holding her close for the drive home.

"Do you feel any different?" he asked, nuzzling her neck.

She made a little soft, contented sound. "I feel like we can take on the world together, if that makes sense."

He chuckled. "It does. I feel that way as well."

"Do your brands hurt?"

He'd never admit it had been much more painful than he'd expected, but it had been worth every ounce of concentration not to make a sound or show that it hurt. Because it *had* hurt. It was good luck for fae to take the brands and not show any signs of the pain to their mate or the witnesses.

"They're well on their way to being healed."

"Could you shift and heal them faster?"

"It's not honorable."

She made a face and then said, "I just realized I've never seen what you look like in your shift."

"Perhaps we can go hunting after we get settled, unless your pack only hunts on the full moon?" Since he hadn't grown up in a pack he had no idea what was acceptable.

"We can hunt in our pack territory anytime we want as long as we go with at least one other person."

"Well, you'll always have me by your side."

Her eyes sparkled with joy.

He said goodbye to the driver and carried her into the house, stopping only long enough to cast the protection spell over the house and lock the front door.

His wolf was chanting in his head, *mine, mine, mine,* and it spilled out of his mouth as he laid his mate gently on the bed.

"Mine."

She lifted her arms, beckoning him to her. "Yours."

He cracked his neck, feeling his wolf close to the surface. "The gown is beautiful. If you want to pass it down to our children, you might want to take it off yourself."

She squeaked in surprise and rolled away. "Don't shred it, I love it!"

He bared his teeth. "What do you love?"

The dress fell from her shoulders, and her breasts were bared to him, the nipples hardening quickly. "You, Crimson. I love you." And then she muttered, "And the dress."

He snarled again, and she giggled, wiggling out of the dress completely and slipping from the bed to drape it over the chair. She wore only white lace panties and the jeweled shoes, standing before him like a goddess.

"Come here, mate," he said, trying not to order her around too much.

She slipped off the shoes and moved to the bed, crawling across it like a cat, nearly purring as she rose to her knees and slipped her fingertips into the waistband of his trousers. If the wolf wasn't riding him so hard, he might have been able to come up with some flowery words or poetry for her, but all he could manage was to not growl with need and shred his own clothes.

Her fingers rubbed against his lower abdomen slowly as she watched him, her eyes darkening with whatever wicked thoughts were running through her mind. She loosened the lacings and pushed the trousers down his hips, tipping her face toward his. Forcing his wolf to the back of his mind so he wouldn't fall on her like an untried youth, he cupped her cheeks and pressed his mouth to hers. The warm scent of her, like flowers and honey mixed together, swirled around them as he teased the seam of her lips with his tongue until she opened them on a sigh. As his tongue delved into her mouth, her hand slipped inside his trousers and stroked his cock. A growl lodged in his throat as she explored him with her delicate hands, and he continued to kiss her, trying not to come just from her light touch and the heady knowledge that they were mates and she was his forever.

His hands trailed over her shoulders and down her arms, tracing the soft curve of her waist as his fingers stroked softly up her stomach to her breasts. He could hear her heart pounding, and it matched the steady, excited thrum of his own. Her skin was soft and warm, silky under his fingers as he traced the underside of her breasts and nibbled her bottom lip. Plumping the lush mounds, he lowered his head and kissed the hard nipples that tipped them. Licking a slow circle around one, he drew it into his mouth slowly. She arched toward him, her fingernails digging into his shoulders as he laved and sucked the tight bud. Tending to the other nipple, he sucked it deeply into his mouth and slipped his hands down her waist. He cupped her pussy with his hand, feeling the heat through the thin fabric, and his wolf howled in happiness. Lifting his mouth to hers, he kissed her like he could climb down inside her, licking and sucking and tasting every hidden place inside the warm recesses of her mouth. His thumb found the hard button of her clit through the fabric and teased it with a light touch. She shivered, moaning softly, and he swallowed the sound like it was food to eat. Her hands had long ago abandoned his cock, but he didn't care. Her touch drove him mad with want.

He felt her drawing close to climax just at the moment she pushed his hand away and collapsed against his chest. "I want to," she spoke between gasps, "come with you inside me. Together."

She leaned away from him and smiled in a soft, sultry way, looking up at him through the veil of her lashes. Nodding, he allowed his claws to slide free of his fingertips, hooked the claws around the waistband of the panties, and ripped them apart. Tossing the fabric aside, he grinned at her surprised look then he stopped thinking altogether as she laid back on their bed and spread her legs, giving him a peek at heaven.

Pink. Glistening. *Mine.*

He bent over to remove his boots, dropping them to the floor with heavy thuds. Shoving his trousers off his legs, he undid the ceremonial leather cuffs from his forearms and laid them on the side table next to the bed. He kissed the tops of both her feet, pushing his prowling wolf to the back again as his claws receded. He wanted to savor this night and give her everything she wanted.

He kissed her calves and her knees, the silky flesh of her thighs, and then he licked her clit and her whole body bucked. Moving up her body with light kisses, he gently rolled her clit between his fingers and thumb, keeping her on the edge of pleasure. Her hands found his shoulders, and her nails dug into his skin as he swirled his tongue around her navel and kissed his way up her stomach. Tugging her clit lightly, he alternated between fast and slow movements, ramping up her pleasure but keeping her from going over.

Her breasts beckoned him, and he licked a circle around her tight nipple, loving the way it hardened a little bit more under his tongue and the way her breath caught in her throat with every stroke. His fingers teased the entrance to her body as his thumb circled her clit, no longer touching the tight bud but teasing the flesh around it.

She whimpered and thrashed under him, whispering his name. He would never tire of the way she said his name when he was loving her. It was like a prayer and a chant rolled together.

Her other nipple beckoned, and he sucked and licked it to hard perfection. Her hands fisted into his hair, and she dragged him up until their lips met. He held himself above her, his hands abandoning their teasing touch as their tongues danced and tangled and bliss settled over him. Supple legs slid over his hips, and he felt the press of her heels against his buttocks as she urged him forward.

Breaking the kiss, he nipped at her bottom lip and looked down between their bodies. His cock was hard, the head glistening with evidence of his arousal, and it seemed to be twitching in an effort to close the distance between them. Their eyes met as he surged forward, burying his cock deeply inside her with one hard press until their bodies met in the sweetest, deepest part of her.

"Oh, Crimson," she moaned, her nails biting into his shoulders as her legs tightened around his hips.

"Lindy," he growled, slipping from her pussy and pushing forward again. Her back arched, and her eyes darkened further, now almost entirely black with the strength of her desire, edged with the amber of her beast. The color was incredible and mesmerizing and held him captive as he moved in and out of her hot, wet depths. She moaned and lifted her hips to meet his, the slow pace he set morphing into a steady, fast thrust and retreat.

He slid one arm underneath her body, lifting her hips at an angle to deepen his thrusts. She groaned loudly, her hands gripping his shoulders even more tightly. He swiveled his hips until she let out a soft sound of pleasure and he knew he'd found the spot to send her over the edge into bliss. He pounded against that same place, driving his body against hers with short, fast strokes as her pussy tightened around his cock like a fist. He wanted her to come. He craved it on a cellular level.

She shrieked as she came, her pussy clamping down on him as her body locked up in the spiral of her pleasure. His wolf howled and he drew her body even closer to his, his fingertips digging into the flesh of her waist where he held her, and he gripped the headboard with his free hand, using the leverage to give her what she needed.

"Oh, Crimson, fuck," she said with a groan, her nails raking down his back as she thrashed under him. He tightened his hold on the climax threatening to overtake him. He wanted her to come again so he could follow her into the abyss.

The headboard smashed against the wall with a loud bang every time he thrust into her, his fingertips gouging the wood as his claws emerged. Sweat slicked their bodies as she clung to him, chanting his name. His fangs elongated in his mouth, and as she moaned, "Yes, yes," his gaze zeroed in on the side of her neck without his marks. Her pussy clutched him as he pumped into her, stroking over the place that would send her into orbit again. He shifted the angle of his body so his pelvis stroked her clit, and she went wild under him, clawing his back and leaning up to sink her teeth into his chest with a throaty moan.

She fell apart on a keening cry, shuddering under him as her eyes rolled back in ecstasy. He let himself go into his climax, howling out his pleasure and filling her body with his seed. Striking quickly while she was lost to the pleasure, he sank his fangs into the unmarked side of her neck and marked her a second time, his whole body trembling as her sweet blood filled his mouth.

Releasing his hold on her neck, he licked the wound to seal it and growled in happiness as she slumped to the mattress with a contented sigh.

"I think you made me melt from the inside out." Her voice was just a whisper but was a balm to his soul.

Nuzzling under her chin, he covered her with his body, careful to keep his weight off her, and breathed deeply the scent of their combined pleasure. She was his entirely now, and he was hers. Body, heart, and soul.

And he'd never been happier.

Chapter Twenty-One

The following afternoon, Lindy lounged on the bed while Crimson packed. They'd been up the entire night, making love again and again, until the sun chased the night from the sky and they'd both passed out. He was everything she'd ever wanted and a bunch of things she hadn't realized were missing from her life.

Two large leather duffels sat open on the bed as he moved from the closet to the bed and back again. He seemed lost in thought, and she let him have the quiet. Besides, he was sexy as hell, and she didn't mind the view.

Earlier that day he'd contacted Commander Fenick and resigned from his position. Giwyn, the evil fairy bitch, was still MIA. But even if she'd been behind bars and awaiting trial, Crimson said he would have wanted to leave the realm anyway. He seemed excited by the prospect of being part of the pack, and she could understand that. There were wolves who chose to leave their packs—they were called rogues—but she couldn't imagine doing that and being without the support of people like her. Even when she had alienated herself from all but the full moon hunts and her best friends, she still wanted to be part of the pack.

He zipped both duffels and said, "I'm ready."

"Then let's go home."

Crimson led her through the house and out into the garden where the fairy ring was waiting. He put the bags down next to several other bags containing more of his belongings and pulled his shirt off, handing it to her. She watched as his wings appeared, pushing through his back and stretching high and wide. He went to his knees and opened the portal then he stood and lifted his bags. As she peered through the portal, she saw the back of her house and smiled. "Your powers are pretty damn cool."

He grinned. "I'm glad you like what I can do."

He refused to let her carry anything, even her own bags, so she stepped through the portal into her backyard and watched as he made several trips between the realms, moving their bags from one side of the portal to the other. He closed the portal and stood looking at it for a long moment. She joined him, sliding her arms around his waist. "I'm happy that you're here with me, Crimson."

"I wouldn't want to be anywhere else."

After they unpacked and made love in the bedroom, she called her friends to say she was home and agreed to meet up with them at Jake's later that evening. She expected at least the higher-ranked males to be at the bar, and it would be a place for Crimson to meet members of the pack in a casual setting.

Lounging on the bed in only a pair of leather pants, Crimson watched her while she got dressed.

"You seem nervous," he said.

"I haven't been to Jake's since I got drunk and pissed off my friends."

"They've forgiven you; you should forgive yourself."

Easier said than done.

"I know. You're just coming face to face with my past at the bar, and it's a little, I don't know, embarrassing?"

In a heartbeat he was at her side and folding her into his arms. "We can stay home. We haven't christened every room in the house yet."

She laughed. "No, I want you to get to know my friends. This is my baggage to deal with, so I will. I don't want to feel like I can't go there whenever we want just because it's been the source of some shameful moments in my past."

She wanted to continue to have new experiences and share them with Crimson. Yes, she'd been to Jake's a thousand times, but she'd never been with a man she loved. She looked up at him and saw the love he had for her, his acceptance of every facet of her life, and it warmed her through and through.

After a thorough kiss, she finished getting ready, and he put one of his tunics on. As they walked out to her car and he opened the driver's door for her, he said, "We should probably go shopping so I can find suitable clothes for your realm."

"We can do that tomorrow. I don't have to go back to work until Monday. But you look amazing." She sat down behind the wheel, and he leaned down and kissed her.

"Do I?"

"You look like a knight with your leather pants and tunic. Very sexy."

He grinned, and it made her stomach flip.

"My lady." He bowed at the waist and her pulse sped up. He gave her a cocky grin and shut the door, striding around the front of her car and climbing into the passenger side. "What is this vehicle called?"

"It's a Ford Mustang. I always wanted one. Have you ever driven a vehicle before?"

As she headed toward Jake's, he told her that his uncle had shown him how to drive, but that he knew he wasn't allowed to legally without a license and some real training.

"When you do get your license, we can share the car. You can drive me to work and then come pick me up."

He took her hand and twined their fingers, resting their joined hands on his thigh. "We'll get all the details figured out later. Tonight, let's just relax and get to know your friends."

She parked in the lot behind Jake's where pack members parked so they could use the back entrance and avoid the line at the front door. He held open the back door for her, and they held hands as they walked down the long hallway leading into the bar. Her heart began to pound as he opened the door that separated the hall and the main bar. She shook off her nerves. She'd made a lot of positive strides over the last few weeks in her personal life. Those who mattered to her—her best friends and Crimson—accepted her for who she was. Although she wanted to be accepted by the pack completely, she was no longer the girl who begged for attention any way she could get it.

Straightening her shoulders, she looked around the bar and found Faith, McKenna, and Drake sitting in one of the circular booths along the wall. Faith waved, and Lindy waved back, leading Crimson through the tables and throng of people.

Faith stood and hugged Lindy. "Welcome home."

"It's good to be home," she said.

Mac wiggled away from Drake to join them, and the three hugged, and then Mac slid back into the booth, and Drake tugged her close. He was frowning. Lindy looked at Mac in question as she slid into the booth and Crimson sat next to her. He put his arm around her shoulders and pulled her into his side.

"There are a lot of unmated males here. Drake doesn't like that," Mac said.

Lindy looked at Crimson who was scanning the bar with intent. Faith snickered. "I don't think Crimson likes it either."

He said, "A good mate watches out for his female at all times."

Lindy smiled broadly. "He's definitely a good mate."

Tina appeared to take their drink order, and Lindy introduced her to Crimson. "Thank you for saving her life."

"It was my honor and duty," Crimson said sincerely.

Tina nodded and took their drink orders. Crimson didn't know what to order since his only experience with mortal beverages had been in Las Vegas where he'd done tequila shots. Drake recommended beer, and Crimson took his advice. When Tina left, there was a brief moment where no one said anything, and then just as quickly as the silence settled it lifted as Mac and Faith demanded to know about her time in the Fae Realm while Drake and Crimson settled into a discussion about the differences between the Fae and Mortal Realms. Lindy loved sitting in the shelter of Crimson's arms and talking to her friends. It was the best of both worlds.

Jason and Michael stopped by the booth to say hello, and Crimson said that he was interested in taking her hunting the following night.

"Why don't you two come to our house? We'll have dinner and go for a run afterward," Jason offered.

Crimson cocked his head. "You eat before you hunt?"

Michael chuckled. "It helps keep us from destroying the small animal population. We all still hunt on the full moon, but with our bellies full, we're not as aggressive."

Jason elbowed him. "You can't say words like belly and aggressive in the same sentence, you sound like a pussy."

Michael rolled his eyes. "You just did."

"Would it be all right if Faith, McKenna, and Drake came as well?" Lindy asked.

"Sure. We'll get some others, too. It's been ages since we've gone out to hunt any other time besides the full moon. It'll be fun. Come over about seven for dinner."

Jason and Michael said goodbye, and as they wandered off to their own booth, the conversations bloomed back to life. Lindy continued with the part of the story where she fell into the brownies' home, and Faith said, "Are you freaking kidding me? That's so cool!"

Lindy snorted. "I could have been sold as a sex slave, dink. Cool isn't the word I'd use for it."

Faith narrowed her eyes. "Come on, admit it. Scary as hell but kinda cool, too."

Laughing loudly, Lindy shook her head. "You're a nut. They're really sweet, though. Maybe you can come to the realm with us sometime and meet them."

"I'd love that."

Eventually Lindy needed to use the restroom, and Faith and Mac accompanied her. They wove through the bar, and she glanced over her shoulder to see Crimson was watching her closely. She swore she could see his eyes flashing to red even from across the bar.

"He's dreamy," Faith said as they walked into the restroom. "You're lucky to have found your truemate."

"You'll find yours when the time is right," Lindy promised.

"Well, he'd better show up soon," Faith grumbled. "My two besties are mated and you'll be popping out babies before long, and I'll be all by my lonesome."

"Whoa, I'm not ready for babies yet," Mac said, straightening her skirt and washing her hands.

"I am," Lindy said. "I can't wait to have Crimson's kids."

"Will they be wolf or fae?" Mac asked as they waited for Faith to finish.

"I don't know. We haven't talked about it. He's both wolf and fae, and I'm all wolf so I have no idea how that will play out genetically. Even if they couldn't shift, it wouldn't matter to me in the least."

"I'll be the best godmother to all your babies and spoil them rotten," Faith promised.

"What's your mom think of things?" Mac asked.

Lindy had called her mom before they came out to the bar and shared the news of her mating and that they were going to be living in Allen permanently. She wasn't really surprised to learn that her mom was packing and getting ready to move away, following a male she believed was her mate.

"She's happy for me, but she's really busy with her own life and said she'll try to visit after she gets settled. I kind of feel like I'm not going to see her for a long time."

"Are you sad?" Faith asked.

"Kind of, but I'm more disappointed that I expected more from her. Her behavior just reminds me of where I was headed myself if I hadn't gotten a wake-up call."

"Crimson would have found you regardless of where you were in your life, though," Mac said. "He did the truemate spell."

"True, but even though I almost died before we met, I'm glad he showed up when he did. I was in a good place, emotionally and mentally."

Mac opened the bathroom door. "Sounds like your wolf in shining armor has good timing."

They walked down the hallway and through the door into the bar, and Lindy's breath gushed from her lungs as she felt herself shoved bodily back through the door and against the wall. For a heartbeat, she couldn't form any words as Bruce pressed her hard against the wood paneling.

"Missed you, bitch," he sneered at her, kicking her legs apart with an aggravated growl.

A claw-tipped hand grabbed Bruce's throat and squeezed tightly as Crimson loomed next to them, his eyes glowing bright red and his fangs elongating in his mouth. With a howl of anger, Crimson tossed Bruce down the hallway, where he landed hard and rolled into the wall.

Crimson swung his gaze to her for only a moment, stroked her cheek gently, and then raced down the hallway with a battle cry that shook the light fixtures. In a blur, Crimson's clothes shredded as he shifted into his wolf form, leaping onto Bruce with a growl. His shifted form was the size of a small horse, and his fur was snow white. He tossed Bruce down the hallway, the male crying out in alarm as he slammed into the wall and fell into a heap on the floor.

"What the hell?" Jason and Michael surrounded Lindy, Jason's mouth agape as he witnessed Crimson pick Bruce up again and throw him against the door leading to the parking lot.

"Bruce attacked me, and Crimson attacked him," Lindy said.

"That's your mate?" Michael asked as Jason slipped in front of Lindy and began to walk down the hallway.

Crimson hit the door with his massive shoulder to open it, and he snapped his jaws around one of Bruce's legs, pulling the shrieking male out into the parking lot.

"Oh shit," Michael hissed.

Lindy was both terrified and elated. Crimson had saved her from whatever Bruce had been planning, but she was worried how far he would take things. Faith and McKenna came through the broken door, their expressions anxious.

Drake, his arms around Mac protectively, said, "What the hell just happened?"

"Bruce, he...attacked me. I don't know what he was going to do, but Crimson is out in the parking lot now." Lindy took off down the hallway, following Jason and Michael as more people began to stream from the door Crimson had broken in his efforts to get to her.

Faith stayed by her side as they raced into the parking lot. A small circle of males stood around Crimson, who was snarling at them, Bruce's bloodied leg between his big jaws.

"Crimson." Jason said his name forcefully. "Don't kill him." Crimson laid his ears back, and a snarl rippled from his throat again.

Just as Lindy pushed through the throng, Crimson crunched down on Bruce's leg, and the bones snapped loudly. Lindy cringed at the sound. Bruce was already unconscious, or he would have been howling. Crimson dropped the broken leg and lifted his head, howling so loudly she had to cover her ears. It was an angry, defiant howl. A challenge.

Jason looked at her. "You need to get your mate and head home, Lindy, let him cool down."

She swallowed hard, and tears stung her eyes. Jason's face softened. "He was protecting you. He didn't do anything wrong. I just didn't want him to kill the bastard, and he didn't. He showed great restraint."

She sniffled and moved to Crimson's side, laying her arm across his furry neck. "How the hell am I going to get you home? You're too big to fit in my car!"

She choked out a laugh and buried her face in his neck, trying not to break down. Bruce had put his hands on her. He certainly hadn't had good intentions.

The fur receded so fast she almost fell to the ground, but then Crimson's strong arms were around her, picking her up and cuddling her close. "I think I fit just fine, *chelle.*"

"You shifted so fast!"

"Of course. The threat," he looked in disdain at the unconscious male Jason and Michael were kneeling next to, "is gone and you needed comfort. Why wouldn't I shift?"

"I can't shift back right away without tremendous effort, it takes a few hours normally."

Jason looked up at them. "I think my dad has some spare clothes in the office if you want to grab something before you head out. I know you were protecting your mate, but thank you for not killing him."

Crimson growled. "I cannot promise I won't kill him the next time I see him."

Michael said, "I think it's time for Bruce to get out of Allen anyway. He's been a pain in the ass for far too long."

Faith said, "Hear, hear."

"I've called Trick, Lindy," Jason said as he stood. "He'll want to get a statement from you both. This is pack business, but he needs to go to the hospital so there will be an inquiry. We'll see you both tomorrow for the hunt."

Jason turned away from them, and Lindy sighed in relief. Trick was the town police officer and mated to one of the she-wolves. He was human, but very protective of the wolf pack, and he had helped them in many ways over the years. Lindy knew Crimson was in no danger of being arrested; Trick would see to that.

"Let's get you some clothes before my mate's head snaps from her trying to look," Drake groused.

"I am *not* trying to look, Drake," Mac said, smacking his shoulder.

"That's because you already *did* look." Faith snickered.

"Love you," Lindy whispered.

"Love you," Crimson answered, kissing her forehead as he followed her friends back into the bar. The crowd was thick, but they parted for the small group, and Lindy didn't bother looking around. The only person in the world she cared about had protected her once more and now, not even concerned with his nudity, was carrying her into the bar. He always thought of her first. She was humbled.

Tina stood next to the open office door and said, "There are some pants and bar T-shirts on the desk, help yourself."

"Thank you," Crimson said, easing inside the office. The door shut, and Crimson put her down slowly. "Are you hurt, *chelle?*"

"No. He just surprised me. I was too shocked to even scream for help because it happened so quickly."

"He is lucky that I only broke his leg. He is a coward for attacking you and a fool for putting his hands on you. In my realm, it would have been within my rights to kill him."

"You could have killed him here, too." Lindy unfolded a T-shirt while he tugged on a pair of jeans. "But there are a lot of humans here tonight who witnessed what happened. When it's just our people, that sort of thing is acceptable, but when humans get involved, they tend to think our ways are animalistic or cruel."

He made a snorting sound. "What he tried to do was cruel and animalistic. What I did was right."

"I'm not arguing with you," she said as he pulled the shirt over his head. "Let's go home."

After giving their statements to Trick, they said goodbye to her friends, and she and Crimson drove home. She was glad to be back within the walls of her house away from the bar.

"Crimson—" she started, but he silenced her with his mouth moving possessively over hers.

His eyes were bright red, and she felt the prick of his fangs against her lips as they descended in his mouth. She could tell he was feeling possessive and needed to get his scent on her and erase the image of Bruce touching her from his mind.

Gripping his hair in her hands, she pulled him away, and he snarled softly, panting. "Make me yours again. I need you so much."

With a body-vibrating growl, he tossed her over his shoulder and stomped down the hallway to the bedroom. He eased her down the front of his body and laid her on the bed, and it was the last thing that he did slowly, as he shredded the clothes from his body and hers, and they made love until dawn.

Chapter Twenty-Two

Crimson watched Lindy dress to go hunting the following evening. He noticed she hadn't put on undergarments before she slipped into shorts and a T-shirt. Earlier that day, she had taken him shopping and bought him a supply of non-fae-realm clothing, buying him a little bit of everything. He didn't like that she had used her own money to buy things for him; it made him feel like a bad mate. The Fae Realm didn't work in the same way as the Mortal Realm where they exchanged paper money for goods and services. In the Fae Realm, they bartered. He had a satchel of gold and gemstones in the drawer in the bedroom; he just needed to find a way to exchange them.

"Why do you not wear undergarments?" He had never worn what she called boxer briefs before, but she had insisted that most people didn't go without undergarments in her realm.

She smiled as she slipped her feet into sandals. "Because when I shift, it's just easier to have fewer clothes to take off and put back on."

He made a face. "I don't know if I like the idea of you being naked in front of other males."

She chuckled. "They're all mated, and I'm all yours."

He decided that he'd make sure her body was shielded with his while she shifted. He held the door of her car open for her and shut it soundly before he got in on the other side. "Do you like it here?" she asked as the engine turned over and she backed the car out of the driveway.

"I like to be anywhere with you."

She winked at him. "I mean do you like the house? It's only a rental; if you don't like it, we can find another house somewhere in town. There are a lot of empty houses available for rent."

He had scouted around the house earlier, and he liked what he saw. It had a nice-sized yard with a wooded area at the back of the property, and it had two empty bedrooms, which he envisioned their children sleeping in.

He put his hand on her thigh, and she pressed her own hand over the top of his. "Why did you pick the house?"

"Well, it's cute. It's got a great kitchen, and I love the brick fireplace in the family room. Plus I like the yard. I enjoy sitting outside on the back patio at night and just looking up at the stars. It's quiet, too. Some of the developments are noisier, lots of wolves hanging out and partying."

He smiled. She'd chosen the house because it appealed to her in several ways. He liked all of those same reasons, but more than that, he liked the house even more now because he knew she had chosen it for a reason.

"What does rental mean?"

"I don't own the house; it's not mine. I pay a certain amount every month to a company that manages the rental properties in town so I can live in the house. There are other homes that are bigger. We could go house hunting."

He shook his head and gave her thigh a little squeeze. "I like the house. Not only because it is nice but because you chose it. I wouldn't want to change anything about where we live."

What he did want to do, though, was find a way to buy the house for her so there was no chance that someone might take it from her. And he needed a job. She worked, and although he would rather she did nothing but stay in bed with him all day, he recognized that things were different in the Mortal Realm and often both males and females in this realm worked.

They arrived at the alphas' home, and there were several other vehicles parked in front of the big house. She took his hand as they walked up the front porch and entered the home, Lindy calling out for her alpha female, who answered they were in the kitchen.

A group of women stood in the kitchen while two young children played on a blanket nearby with a pile of toys. The males were outside on the deck.

"Come and meet everyone," the alpha female, Cades, said. And then she began to introduce the mates of the males. Karly, Shyne, Reika, and Jenna all smiled and greeted him warmly and hugged Lindy. Faith and McKenna were also in the kitchen and joined them. "The guys are outside, Crimson, if you want to join them for a few minutes before the meal."

He kissed Lindy on the cheek and walked out to the deck and greeted Jason, who introduced him officially to the other males. Michael, who he had met previously, was mated to the human female, Shyne, and was pack second. Linus was fourth in rank and was mated to Karly, who was not human or wolf, but something called an Angel Mate. Reika was the pack healer and mated to Bo, who was pack third. Logan was the fifth ranked, a huge male with tribal tattoos covering his arms, and Crimson could smell the fae on him and knew that his mate was the she-fae, Jenna.

Drake, who looked thrilled to be included in the hunt with the older males, said, "We were just talking about the male you roughed up last night."

Crimson growled.

Jason chuckled. "He's still in the hospital. Michael contacted his family, who are not from around here, and they're coming to take him home. When he's conscious, I'll exclude him officially from the pack, and he can be some other alpha's problem."

Linus said, "The single females in the pack will want to throw a parade for you for helping to get rid of the bastard."

"He was unpleasant to females other than my Lindy?"

Bo nodded. "He's always been very aggressive. He settled down some once Cades took over as alpha female, but the females in the pack will definitely breathe easier with him gone."

Crimson was glad the male was going to be leaving. He had not been joking when he said he would kill him if he saw him again. As it was, he was currently tempted to find the hospital and break his other leg.

He looked at the alpha and said, "May I speak with you privately?"

"Sure," Jason said and led him to the other side of the deck.

"I want to buy the house that Lindy is renting so that no one will take it from her."

Jason looked confused. "No one is going to take it from her."

"She told me about renting it; that it doesn't belong to her. I want to change that."

He grinned. "I get that. Sure, you just need money. I have no idea if you guys have the same money system as we do."

"I have gold and gems to exchange, but I don't know where to do it, and I want to surprise her so I haven't asked."

"There's a place about a half hour from here that does exchanges like that, and the owner is a friend of my dad's and will give you a fair deal. We can go tomorrow if you'd like. I'll just tell your mate that I'm talking to you about a job."

Crimson frowned. "I don't want to lie to her."

"Oh, it won't be a lie. I was asked by the retirement community director to find out if you'd like to be in charge of the security guards. Lindy told Cades you were a soldier in the military in the Fae Realm, and Jenna said that you're even more powerful than a normal fae because you're a *wulfen*. The male who was in charge of the guards moved away about a year ago, and the position was never filled, so the director's husband is handling things, but he's bitching because he's retired and doesn't want to work anymore. After we go to the exchange place, we can stop by the retirement community. It's important to me that the security is managed well. My parents and grandfather live there. Our kid stays over sometimes." Jason sighed and glanced out over the yard and into the woods. "It's safe in Allen, but times are changing. Someone is laying traps inside our territory. It's not a far leap to know that our retirement community, although gated, is vulnerable because the security force is not well trained or led properly."

"I'd be honored. I was captain in the military and have been training since I was a child."

"Maybe you can teach some self-defense classes and that kind of thing at the community center after you guys get settled." He cleared his throat, and Michael appeared next to him. "On the full moon, we'll join you and Lindy as official mates. You'll be inducted into the pack. Normally, when a male joins the pack, there are ranking fights held on the following full moon so you can find your place in the pack. But I'd like to ask you if you'd be willing to take a special place within the pack."

"What did you have in mind?"

Jason looked at Michael, who said, "In the old days—by which I mean old *old* days—the mates who weren't able to participate in the hunt for whatever reason—age, pregnancy, injury—were guarded by a *Fylax*. He was a personal guard to the mates, the fiercest and deadliest male."

Jason said, "We'd like to ask you to become our *Fylax*. It's a position of honor, unranked within the pack, so you wouldn't have to fight for position. The Tressel Pack hasn't had a *Fylax* in several generations. It used to be that a male was chosen each generation to be trained especially for the position, but like many of our traditions, it fell to the wayside. We'd be honored if you would accept the position."

Currently, Jason said, the mates and children were guarded by a small group of females who waited for a few hours until the males came home, and then they went out and hunted for the remainder of the night. Lindy had mentioned she had been guarding the alpha female the night he had spelled for her.

"Instead of having rotating guards, we want to implement permanent guards. Lindy can become one, as can Drake and his mate, McKenna, and Faith. Until Faith finds a mate, my mom has offered to become the sixth guard."

The other males joined them, and Logan said, "It makes my wolf crazy to be away from Jenna on the full moon, but if I don't hunt, then I get agitated, and that's not good for anyone. I'll feel safer knowing that a well-trained male like you is watching over her and the other non-shifting mates."

An overwhelming sense of belonging filtered through him. Emotion welled up inside him. His whole life he'd wanted to be with people like himself, but he hadn't thought that would ever be possible.

"I'd like to talk to Lindy about it, but I'd be honored."

The males whooped a cheer, and Crimson laughed. Jason clapped him on the back. "Fucking awesome."

Logan said, "*Resh*, Jason. Faes say '*resh*'."

"Right, right," Jason said. "*Resh*."

He went into the house to find Lindy and shared the news with her. "Really?" she asked in surprise. "That's wonderful! Do you want to do it?"

Snaking his arms around her, he looked down into her pretty blue eyes and said, "If you're okay with it, then I am. We'll get to guard the mates and pups together, and when you're carrying my pups, I'll get to watch over you. Sounds like a win-win situation to me."

"Me, too." She snuggled into him with a happy sigh. "Just how many pups are we talking about?"

"I don't know," he said, "is *tons* a good number?"

She laughed and tipped her face up to his for a kiss, which he gladly gave.

After their meal, the group headed out to hunt. The mates wished them a good hunt, and he held Lindy's hand as they walked back to what she referred to as the "full moon meeting place." The large clearing had a firepit in the center that was lit on the full moon. Darkness had descended, but wolves could see better in the dark than humans, and they had no trouble navigating the woods.

When the group began to strip, Crimson pushed Lindy behind a large tree. "I don't want anyone to see you naked but me."

"They're my pack. We've been seeing each other naked for years, it's no big deal."

His wolf didn't much care for that, and he snarled. "It's a big deal now."

She laid her hand on his neck and stroked her thumb on his pulse. "I'm sorry, you're right. I don't really want anyone to see you naked either."

He watched her strip behind the safety of the tree and was mesmerized as her body changed from beautiful human to lovely wolf. He'd never watched another wolf shift before. She shook herself out and made a soft, growling sound, bumping his leg. Quickly stripping, he shifted into his form. He was much bigger than she was, and he made a mental note to his wolf not to outrun her because his legs were so much longer than hers.

With a chuff, he nuzzled her neck and inhaled her scent. The sweet scent of her made his wolf salivate, and he wanted to sink his fangs into her neck to mark her in this form, too. But he had no idea if wolves did that. She licked his cheek and motioned with her head to follow her, and they met up with the other wolves in the center of the clearing. The wolves all froze and stared at him, and he realized that some of them had not seen him in his shift.

The silence was broken after a long moment when Jason barked sharply, and the wolves snapped to attention and took off as a group. Crimson kept his stride short so he didn't pass Lindy by and stayed close to her as they followed Jason, who led the pack on the hunt. The scents and sounds of the woods surrounded him. He smelled birds and small animals and heard the sound of the packs' paws hitting the ground rhythmically as bushes and tree limbs rustled with animals making their getaways. Jason increased his stride, so Lindy and Crimson did as well, as the group twisted and turned through the woods.

The pack wheeled to the right as Crimson heard the distant sound of hoof beats and knew they were following deer, and his heart rejoiced at a real hunt with wolves. He couldn't wait to show Lindy that he was a worthy mate in both forms.

At the moment the deer came into view, a tingling sensation descended Crimson's spine, and every nerve ending in his body screamed *danger*! He scanned the area quickly, and he sensed something was out of the ordinary in the dark woods. Leaning to the left, he snagged Lindy's scruff and pulled her to a quick stop with a loud growl. She whined and then went still as Crimson's eyes roamed around the area. The wolves had left them behind, but not for long, as he heard the sound of them coming back toward them. Crimson shifted into his human form and raised his hand. His palm glowed brightly as his fire abilities allowed him to hold a small flame in his hand to shed light on the area.

Glinting under some leaves was a trap. The same kind of deadly trap that had almost killed his mate. Rage boiled up inside him as he realized that Lindy had almost run into the trap the others had miraculously missed.

Jason shifted. "Fuck me, how did you know that was there?" He lifted the leaves from the trap carefully to expose it.

"I sensed it."

Lindy leaned against his leg, whining softly. He rested his free hand on the top of her head.

"We can't figure out who's leaving the traps. It smells like the woods. I think they're coating it with some kind of artificial scent that keeps us from detecting it. The first trap we found had fresh meat on it, but the trap that caught Lindy and this one are empty."

Michael, who had also shifted, said, "The traps keep getting closer and closer to our full moon meeting place, Jas. Who the fuck is leaving them?"

Jason looked at Crimson. "Do you want to help us capture the fuck that's leaving these things?"

"Of course."

"Good. Logan and Linus, take the others and head back to the house. Be careful." Logan, still in his wolf form, chuffed and waited for Faith, McKenna, and Drake to join him. Crimson squatted down and kissed Lindy's snout. "Stay close to them. I'll be back soon when the threat is gone." He didn't want her to be apart from him, but he knew that Logan and Linus were fierce males and would see them safely back to the alphas' home.

She whined in protest but seemed to accept what he said, and after licking his chin, she trotted over to the others and left. Jason said, "You can shift back into your form again, right? Because I've got an idea."

Jason relayed his plan to them, and after some preparations, the plan went into action. Crimson disabled the trap the same way he had manipulated the one that had captured Lindy. Then he shifted into his wolf form and lay down on his side, and Jason carefully arranged the broken trap around his back leg to make it appear that he had been caught.

Bo appeared a few minutes later with a dead rabbit between his jaws. Jason ripped the flesh of the rabbit open and rubbed its blood along Crimson's white fur to mimic a wound.

"However long it takes, we'll be right here," Jason said. He and Michael turned to the nearby trees. Each one scaled a tree on either side of Crimson and climbed high until they were obscured by the leaves. Bo slinked back into the shadows and slipped underneath a thick bush. As instructed, Crimson began to howl in distress.

The night passed slowly. Crimson howled a few times each hour, but otherwise listened intently for the sounds of someone approaching. Dawn came, the sun cutting through the trees and warming him as he lay prone with the trap around his leg. He was restless and wanted to shift back into his human form, but he knew how important it was to find whoever was laying the traps and put a stop to it. He couldn't abide his mate or his pack being harmed.

He smiled inwardly. He had a pack now. *Resh.*

He distantly heard a twig snap and made himself appear to be unconscious. He hadn't raised his voice to howl in about an hour.

"Well, well," a rough male voice said, "lookie what the trap caught."

Three males came into the clearing. Their bodies stank of alcohol mixed with body odor, and it took all his willpower not to wrinkle his nose in disgust.

"I ain't never seen such a big wolf before," a thin, reedy voice said.

"No matter. We'll call him a rare species and get a good price for the pelt."

"But I thought there was people inside them wolves?" another, younger voice said.

"Not when they're dead. The law says if they die in their wolf forms that they're wolves and we can do what we want to with them. Skeet, go check his pulse," the rough voice said.

"You go do it!" the reedy-voiced one said.

"Harry said we was supposed to leave the dead wolves in the traps as a warning," the younger voice said.

"I need the money," the rough voice said. "And they'll get the hint anyway when one of their animals goes missing."

A bird sounded high above them and Crimson knew it was not a real bird, but Jason's signal. In a blink, Crimson shifted into his fae form, his wings sprouting from his back quickly as he manifested his sword. Jason and Michael landed on the ground on either side of the small group of hunters, and Bo joined them, growling angrily.

Crimson pointed his sword at the center male. All three were as white as sheets, their mouths gaped open in shock.

Jason growled, "Why are you laying traps in my pack's territory?"

The center one gathered himself and made a disgusted face. "You animals don't own property. These here woods are for anyone to hunt in."

"The law," Jason ground out through clenched teeth, "states that my pack's territory is private property and no humans may hunt on it without my express permission as Alpha. Since I've never seen your ugly face before, I know you didn't get my permission."

Bo snarled loudly and lunged at the younger male, who fell backward onto his butt and started to cry. "Don't let him kill me, please! It was Harry Smith who hired us."

The center male kicked at the young male. "Shut your hole, Jerry."

"I don't want to get eaten!" the young male wailed.

Crimson stepped closer and sent a flame up the blade of the sword that swirled and danced along the metal. He could see the sweat beading up on the male's skin as he closed the distance between them.

"You will tell my alpha everything, or I will carve you into pieces and leave them on your mother's porch."

The fire along the blade began to blister the male's skin, and although he appeared to want to stand firm, he shouted, "Okay, okay! I'll tell, just don't kill me!"

Jason said, "Stand down, Crimson. I think you made your point."

Crimson stepped back so Jason could get in front of the three males, raising his flaming sword high enough to light the area well. Within minutes, the males had shared the story of the traps, that they had been hired by a local farmer who wanted to scare the pack away from town and force them to settle in another area.

"For what purpose?" Jason demanded.

The center male, who had lost all his bravado, said, "I don't know, Harry never said. He just said that if a few of you got hurt you'd take off."

Jason stepped closer and gripped both males who stood before him around their throats. They struggled, but Jason's grip was far too tight. Their faces turned red, and their eyes bulged as he cut off their air. "You came onto my territory. You terrorized my people. You injured my wolf. By rights, I could kill you now." The threat hung heavily in the air for several moments as the hunters' eyes widened with fear, and the scent of urine filled the air as their bladders emptied. One of the males' eyes rolled back in his head, and he fainted. Jason dropped him to the ground, and Crimson saw his fingers flex tighter on the throat of the remaining male. As his face turned purple, he stopped struggling, and Jason dropped him.

The youngest of the three was still on the ground, blubbering that he didn't want to die and he was sorry. Jason told the male to shut up, and he did with a squeaking sound, trembling from head to toe as he curled up into a ball.

Jason said to Crimson, "Can you get back to my house quickly and have Cades call Trick at the police station and then lead him and his people out here? I don't want to take these assholes anywhere near my house."

Crimson nodded, released his sword so it disappeared, and lifted into the air with a flap of his wings. He moved through the woods quickly, stopping at the clearing and picking up his pants, and racing on to the alphas' home. He landed behind a tree at the edge of the backyard and tugged the pants on, and then walked the rest of the way to the house. Lindy, dressed in borrowed clothes, was waiting on the porch for him and leapt into his arms. He carried her into the house and relayed the message to Cades, who pulled her cell from her pocket and dialed.

Standing inside the kitchen, Crimson waited with Lindy, Cades, Linus, Faith, McKenna, Drake, and Logan. The mates and the two children were still sleeping, camped out in the front room. The police showed up, and Crimson led them to the hunters in the woods where the males were arrested and then taken to jail, while the farmer who'd hired them, Harry Smith, was arrested as well.

Crimson and Lindy went home after the males were arrested and taken away, and Jason called later in the afternoon to share the story of the hunters.

"Harry spilled his guts pretty quickly when faced with jail. His brother-in-law is a developer and said that the pack's territory is prime real estate and could be turned into upscale homes on small parcels of land. Apparently there is a market for luxury homes in small towns. At any rate, the territory belongs to the Tressel Pack, and the only way it can be purchased is if the pack leaves the area. Then we would forfeit the land, and it would be sold at auction. His brother-in-law told him that if he could get us to leave, Harry could buy up the land and then sell it to his brother for a tidy profit."

"So he hired the hunters to set the traps, knowing that wolves could be killed by them," Crimson said.

"Pretty much. He told Trick he didn't know the traps were deadly, but no one believes him. The hunters are trying to roll on Harry to get less time in jail, and Harry is trying to lay the blame on the hunters, but they're all going away for a long time. It's a federal offense to lay traps on shifter territory."

Crimson didn't understand the male's desire for money that could blind him to hurting innocents.

Jason said, "He was never our biggest fan, but he's been in town since I was a kid, and we thought he lived in peace with us. I guess some people are really good at hiding their true feelings."

"I'm glad he's gone," Crimson said.

"Me, too. We're going to do a sweep of the area tomorrow, and I'd like you to help. It will take all day, but afterward we can visit the man I told you about and then discuss your job prospects."

Crimson smiled inwardly. "Sounds like a plan."

The night of the full moon, Crimson found himself nervous for the first time in a long while. He could stand at the front lines in battle without breaking a sweat, but the mating and induction ceremonies for the pack were filling him with nerves. He and Lindy had spent the entire day in bed, and it had been a sweet, sweet day of sharing pleasure. His wolf, far more content than he'd ever been, had reveled in the love of his mate, and he looked forward to hunting with her once more.

When it was nearly time to head to the alphas' home for the pre-hunting cookout, Lindy slipped from the bed with a groan and gave him an impish smile before walking into the bathroom and shutting the door. He quickly donned a pair of jeans and a shirt and grabbed an envelope and a small box from underneath the stack of jeans in the closet. By the time she came out of the bathroom, he was sitting on the bed once more, waiting.

Her steps slowed, and she looked at him curiously.

"Get dressed, *chelle*, and then we need to talk."

Her brows arched, but she simply nodded and walked into the closet. She came out a few moments later wearing shorts and a shirt.

"My father told me once that males who couldn't provide for their mates were unworthy males, lower than the lowest *scrugbeetle*." He patted the space on the mattress next to him, and she sat down. "Our home in the Fae Realm had been my father's before he mated my mother, and I had few needs, so I saved my earnings for the future." From inside the envelope, he pulled out a clipped stack of paperwork. "Jason was kind enough to take me to a broker who helped me exchange my earnings for the money of your realm, and I used it to buy two things."

He handed her the papers, and she looked down at the top page. Confusion flitted across her features. "This is a deed with my name on it."

"I bought the house for you."

"What?" Her eyes rounded in surprise, and her grip tightened on the papers.

"I went to the mortgage company and made arrangements to buy the house for you. These papers mean that the house is yours and no one can take it from you."

Her mouth opened then closed, and she made a soft, squeaking sound as tears glistened in her eyes. She threw herself into his arms and buried her face in his neck. "You didn't have to do this for me, Crimson," she whispered thickly, "but thank you."

He squeezed her tightly, and a small growl of contentment rippled through him. "I did have to do it. I want to provide for you and any pups we have. I don't want to be a bad mate. I want to take care of you in every way. Make you feel safe and secure in our future."

She eased away, and he brushed the tears from her cheeks. "I do feel safe with you. And I love you so much. Thank you." She sniffled. "But the deed should have your name on it, too."

"It will." He smiled. Slipping to the floor on his knees, he opened the box that contained a diamond ring flanked with rubies and emeralds and said, "Will you marry me, Lindy? Will you share my name, my future, my life? My heart is yours forever."

Fresh tears slipped down her cheeks as she let him put the ring on, fell into his lap with a resounding "Yes!", and kissed him.

His wolf growled happily and Crimson shared in the beast's excitement. Their mate was agreeing to be theirs in every possible way. Once they were officially joined by the pack and then married by human standards, she would be his forever, and he would be hers.

At one time, Crimson hadn't thought much about his future outside of his military service. Now, his future was filled with thoughts of taking care of his mate and their future pups. He couldn't wait for what would come.

Chapter Twenty-Three

Lindy's left hand trembled in Crimson's as Jason wound the mating strap around them, joining them officially as mates within the pack. She'd never been so nervous in her life. She must feel how a bride felt when she walked down the aisle, like it was a dream, and she might wake up at any second.

Crimson squeezed her hand slightly and smiled at her. His eyes were red, the same color as the rubies on her engagement ring, and she saw a hint of his fangs as he smiled at her. Jason spoke the words of the mating ceremony, and Lindy and Crimson responded, vowing themselves to each other for the span of their lives.

Crimson pulled her toward him, their captive hands pressed tightly between them, and growled, "mine" before he kissed her deeply. The pack howled and cheered, and Lindy was happy that the pack was so accepting of her mate and their joining.

Jason unwound the mating strap and gave the long piece of leather to Lindy, who folded it and tucked it into her pocket. She stepped away, joining Faith and Mac with the pack as Jason officially offered the position of *Fylax* to Crimson. He accepted, and the pack cheered once more. Lindy had never heard of the guardian position of *Fylax* before, but she was thrilled there was a place for her mate within the pack and that he was happy with it. And she was also happy that she was now one of the permanent mate guards and could join Crimson each full moon to watch over the mates, until she became pregnant and couldn't shift any longer, and then he would guard her and their pups as well.

"What are you thinking about with that silly grin on your face?" Faith asked.

"Pups."

"Man, I need to get mated," Faith grumbled, and Lindy laughed, joining Crimson as Jason called for the pack to shift and wished everyone a good hunt.

Crimson pushed her gently behind a tree and kissed her, tugging on the hem of her top. Their kiss broke, and he pulled it off her quickly and smiled with a soft growl. "You are so beautiful."

"You're not so bad yourself, sexy." She grinned at his amazing upper body as he tossed his shirt to the ground to join hers.

"We have a job to do, and then we can hunt together. This time, without worry of traps."

"And then we can go home."

"Where I will enjoy celebrating our mating night by making you scream my name. A lot."

She loved his sexy threats.

They stripped and shifted together, and she nuzzled the thick snow-white fur of his neck and inhaled the spicy scent of him. He was bigger than her, more like a small horse than a wolf, but he was all hers. Every gorgeous inch.

With a chuff, she followed him to where the mates stood with the other guards, and they followed them back to the alphas' house. While the mates and two small children went into the house, Crimson left Lindy at the back porch and swept the perimeter, arranging the other guards around the house. He nuzzled her neck and then loped off to the edge of the woods where he paced the length of the property, listening and watching for danger. It filled Lindy with pride to know that her mate was such a great guard, so careful in his duties. When she joined the mates in the home with her first pregnancy, whenever that would be, she would rest easy knowing her mate was watching over her. She was pretty sure there was no guard fiercer than a *wulfen* watching over his mate and pups.

The night sped by quickly, and when the males returned from the hunt, the guards gathered in the yard and went off to hunt together. Lindy loved racing through the woods with Crimson as he shortened his gait so that he didn't outpace her. She was pretty fast, but he had legs that were twice as long as hers, which meant he could run circles around her.

They caught the scent of a herd of deer deep in the pack's territory, and with a few simple, barked commands, Crimson and Lindy branched off as the others went a different direction. Lindy and Crimson would stalk the herd from one direction while the four others would chase the deer right into their waiting jaws. Lindy had never hunted like this before, and it was exciting. Her fur bristled, and she salivated with the thought of sharing a kill with her mate.

As they waited in the darkness, the air shimmered in front of them suddenly, a bright light seeming to rend the darkness before them. Crimson growled and pushed Lindy behind him as a portal opened and the crazy she-fairy Giwyn stepped out of the portal. Lightning sparked from her fingertips, and her eyes glowed neon blue. She was speaking a spell of some sort, and Crimson shifted into his fae form, manifesting his sword.

Just as he swung his sword down, the thundering of hooves filled the air, and Giwyn screamed in alarm as Lindy's packmates chased a herd of deer right into the she-fairy. Crimson grabbed Lindy around the torso and lifted into the air, flapping his wings to carry her out of danger. She watched as Giwyn was trampled, the lightning sparking a few times before being snuffed out as her screams were cut off, replaced with a loud, gurgling sound.

Four wolves, eyes wide with shock, stared at the broken body of the fairy. They shifted as a group as Crimson set Lindy down on the ground and she shifted into her human form. Crimson knelt and checked Giwyn's pulse and shook his head.

Tina gasped. "Who was she? We didn't see her until the deer had already knocked her down."

Crimson spat angrily, "She was the female who had my mate kidnapped in my realm. She is evil." He glanced at Lindy and stood, shielding her nudity with his body. "She was casting a spell that would have rendered us both unconscious. I have no doubt that she planned to kill us both."

Lindy shivered and hugged herself closer to him. "I'm glad she's dead, but I'm sorry she had to die so violently. No one deserves to be trampled to death."

He snarled but said nothing, resting his cheek on top of her head and pulling her even closer.

Tina said, "I'll go get Jason. We need to do something with the body."

"I'll take her to my commander, and they will deal with it. I just need some damn clothes first."

Tina smiled, but it was shaky. "I'll bring them back for you all."

A half hour later, Lindy and Crimson went through a portal that Crimson created. The one Giwyn had come through had evaporated when she died. They left the body with Commander Fenick who would see that it was returned to her family so they could bury her. When they returned to the Mortal Realm, the portal opened in her backyard, and she stepped out then turned to watch him come through and close the portal. His wings receded into his back, and he turned and picked her up in his arms.

"I believe we had plans, my sweet mate."

"Naked plans?" she asked.

"*Very* naked plans."

She kissed him and snuggled closer, thankful for her mate. It seemed impossible that she had come to such a wonderful place in her life after such hardship. She'd created a life for herself where she'd been reviled by the pack and had been digging herself out of the mess she'd made when she found her mate. Now, they were both accepted, even by those who had seemingly hated her before. The younger males had apologized profusely, and while she was certain that, in part, it had been because they were afraid of her big, bad mate, she accepted their apologies with grace.

In the span of a few weeks, she'd been nearly killed by a trap, rescued by her truemate, kidnapped by an evil wizard and nearly sold into sexual slavery, rescued by brownies, and mated in an amazing ceremony in front of an entire city of fae. She'd found her place in her pack as a guard, and her mate had been accepted by her packmates as one of their own. Her mate had shown her it didn't matter what form your mate was, whether wolf or human or fae, it only mattered that love was freely given.

She'd never had a place where she felt loved and safe and respected all at the same time, but Crimson had turned their modest house into just such a place. Where they loved, protected, and respected each other. She had a home now, and it was all thanks to her *wulfen* and the night he'd spelled for her.

Epilogue

One Year Later

Cadence pushed the pink candle shaped into a number two into the pink frosting of her daughter's birthday cake, humming the birthday song under her breath. Outside in the yard, bunches of pink and white balloons were tied onto the deck railing, and an enormous bouncy princess castle sat out in the yard. Pack members milled in the yard, finding shade under a big tent. Karly had catered the birthday party, making Lyric's favorite breaded chicken bites and macaroni and cheese and other dishes for the adults.

Shyne came into the kitchen carrying her newborn son, Micah. "That cake is freaking amazing."

"Mrs. B. is really talented. Lyric told her she wanted a wolf princess cake, and that's exactly what she got." Mrs. B., who was an extraordinary baker who worked at Lonestar's and was Karly's friend, had made the cake in the shape of a wolf sitting on its haunches, wearing a sparkling tiara, a jeweled necklace, and matching bracelets.

Micah made a squeaking sound, and Cades looked up to see Michael stride into the kitchen. "There's my boy." He grinned, lifting the little bundle from Shyne's arms. He turned and carried his son right out of the kitchen, and Shyne laughed.

"He's the best dad. I love how they are together. Yesterday I found Michael asleep on the hammock on the back porch with Micah sleeping on his chest. Too adorable."

Cades rubbed her four-month baby belly, knowing that Jason was hopeful their next child would be a boy.

"I never doubted Michael would be a great dad. They both had good influences growing up between Peter and their grandfather," Cades said.

All of the males in the pack seemed to be good dads, and it amazed Cades to think of how much the pack had grown just in the last year. Besides welcoming Crimson into the pack, Faith had mated a wolf named Liam from another pack. When Liam had brought his brother, Garrett, to the joining ceremony, Garrett and Sunny realized that they were meant to be mates. So Faith, who was an only child, got not only her mate at the joining ceremony but a brother and sister-in-law. Half the females in the pack were pregnant or nursing, and both Cades and Karly were pregnant as were Lindy, McKenna, Faith, and Jenna. Reika, whose son had been born in the spring, said she was pretty sure there was something in the water. And Cades was beginning to believe that. But according to her mother-in-law, Tina, wolf packs tended to grow in leaps and bounds in this way, with the next generation of pack members being born close together.

Since she was an only child herself, she was glad that Lyric was going to have a sibling soon and that she would soon have other kids to play with in the near future. Right now it was just Lyric and Karly's son, Remy, who was a few months older than her. They were very close, the older boy already protective of her daughter even though they were still so young, and she was glad Lyric would never know what it was like to be excluded.

The pack would be Lyric's extended family as it had become Cades, and someday her daughter might join with her mate and take over the pack, or the honor might fall to Cades and Jason's son, if they had one. But it didn't really matter. She just wanted Lyric to be happy, and she was glad to be surrounded by her friends and family in the pack.

Jason looked in the open back door. "The natives are restless, sweet."

"Coming, coming," she said and then looked around the table. "Oh, shoot, I don't have matches."

Lindy called from the deck, "Crimson can help."

"He's so handy." Shyne laughed.

Cades carried the cake out onto the porch, and Crimson, whose arm was around Lindy's shoulder protectively, just looked at the candle, and it blazed to life. She thanked Crimson and carried the cake down the steps to the tent where the pack was gathering to sing happy birthday to her daughter.

She set the cake down in front of her daughter, who sat at the head of a long table wearing a sparkling crown and a frilly pink sundress. As Cades put the cake down in front of her daughter and the pack began to sing, she smiled in happiness at her daughter and her mate and the friends and pack members who made up her extended family.

Her mate, her daughter, her baby on the way…she was one happy hybrid she-wolf and felt incredibly blessed. As Lyric blew out the candle and stuck her hand into the cake, the pack cheered, and Jason pulled Cades close. "I love you, my mate."

"I love you, too, my alpha."

The world dropped away as Jason's mouth captured hers for a kiss that made her toes curl. She wouldn't change a thing about her life, and she looked forward to what the future held for her, her family, and her pack.

The End

Contact the Author

Website: http://www.rebutlerauthor.com
Email: rebutlerauthor@gmail.com
Twitter: @rebutlerauthor
Facebook: www.facebook.com/R.E.ButlerAuthorPage

Also from R. E. Butler

Wiccan-Were-Bear Novella Series
A Curve of Claw
A Flash of Fang
A Price for a Princess
A Bond of Brothers
A Bead of Blood
A Twitch of Tail
A Promise on White Wings

The Wolf's Mate Series
The Wolf's Mate Book 1: Jason & Cadence
The Wolf's Mate Book 2: Linus & The Angel
The Wolf's Mate Book 3: Callie & The Cats
The Wolf's Mate Book 4: Michael & Shyne
The Wolf's Mate Book 5: Bo & Reika
The Wolf's Mate Book 6: Logan & Jenna
The Wolf's Mate Book 7: Lindy & The Wulfen

The Necklace Chronicles
The Tribe's Bride
The Gigolo's Bride

Ashland Pride Series
Seducing Samantha (Ashland Pride One)
Loving Lachlyn (Ashland Pride Two)
Marking Melody (Ashland Pride Three)

Hyena Heat Series
Every Night Forever (Hyena Heat One)
Every Dawn Forever (Hyena Heat Two)

Wilde Creek Series
Mate of Her Heart (Book One)
The Alpha's Heart (Book Two)

COMING IN 2014...
Redeeming Rue (Ashland Pride Book 4)

As an albino black panther banished by her people, Veruka Jennings knows if her clan discovers she had a child, it would mean death for them both. Labeled an abomination and forbidden from having cubs, she's spent the better part of her life as an outcast, believing she is worthless because of the color of her fur. After secretly overhearing traveling clan members discuss a bonding ceremony in Indiana, she decides to spy on the proceedings for one last look at the people who treated her like trash.

When James and John Fallon investigate a shadowy figure in the woods during a bonding ceremony, they do not expect to find the woman they are meant to share. But instead of enjoying their mating, they are embroiled in a clan war as they fight to protect Veruka and her son, who have come to mean everything to them. If they can protect her, will they be able to keep her? Or will Rue believe she's not worthy of their love and disappear from their lives forever?

Warning: This book contains one spunky heroine who will do anything to keep her son safe, two males who aren't about to let the slippery female get away, and a ticked off clan of panthers who want bloody revenge for their broken laws. Expect plenty of growls and snarled curses, love bites, ceremonial mating, and scorching m/f/m loving that only happens when two mountain lions finally find the woman of their dreams. Contains m/f/m interaction.

Every Sunset Forever (Hyena Heat Three)

Raised by wolves, were-hyena Whisper Callahan has spent the better part of her life struggling to fit into a world where she's the odd one out. Her adopted family loves her, of that she has no doubt, but now they're encouraging her to connect with her own kind. At an annual gathering of unmated were-hyenas in Pennsylvania, Whisper finds herself torn between the past she never knew and the family that raised her as their own.

Were-hyenas Nyte, Azrael, and Fade don't expect much to come from the *gathering* except a few days off from work at Stone's Gym in Dalton, Kentucky. They don't expect to follow the sound of tears and find their mate crying in the woods. And they certainly don't expect to find themselves trying to protect her from her own family while she comes to terms with all that she learns about herself and her past. But hyenas are nothing if not protective of their mates, and they're willing to do whatever it takes to keep her safe. And keep her forever.

It wouldn't be a Hyena Heat novel without plenty of hot m/f/m/m loving, three males that would do anything for their mate, and a female that is in need of love. Expect plenty of possessive behavior and excessive use of the word "mine."

Made in the USA
Lexington, KY
01 May 2015